Bend Foot Bailey

BY POTBAKE PRODUCTIONS

90 Days of Violence
Forward Ever! Backward Never!
oOh My Testicles!
Boy Days

Bend Foot Bailey

Michael Cozier

Potbake Productions
Trincity, Trinidad and Tobago

Books may be ordered by contacting:

Potbake Productions
#3, 3rd Street West,
Beaulieu Avenue,
Trincity,
Trinidad,
West Indies
www.potbake.com
(868)640-3724
(868)487-9115
(868)731-0209

First published by Potbake Productions
ISBN: 978-976-95236-5-4

Thanks to my entire family and my friends; without you all I'll be utterly lost. To the villagers of Icacos, Fullerton and Cedros: you were a part of me growing up. To Lyndon, my nephew, who is also my editor and friend. To all the people who were brave enough to read my first book. A special thank you to the workers of Trinmar: you have given me the confidence to continue. To Caribbean people everywhere: you occupy a very special place in my heart. To the West Indies cricket team: you have inspired me ever since I was a little boy. And to God, without whom we are nothing.

Dedicated to my sister Cynthia.

Contents

The Point Fortin Debt Collector

I was working with a small contractor fellar down on Trident Base. The man getting little odd jobs out on the platforms, a little painting here, a little welding and fabricating there, and things was going all right. Then one morning the boss came with a bright smile.

'I get the big one, boys.'

'What big one?' the five of us asked.

'The landing stage on Platform E!' he exclaimed – the boys let out a jubilant 'WHOOP!'

Well the first mistake the boss make is he hire a Grenadian fellar and put him in charge of the work. You know Grenadians can't measure and on top of that the man ignorant to boot. He not taking advice from anybody. If you tell him anything he cursing you in his heavy Grenadian accent. Well under the iron supervision of the Grenadian, we cut, chop, weld and fabricate and when we take the landing stage out on a barge and try to hook it up to Platform E, nothing meshing up at all. The Trident Supervisor, a fellow named John G Kennedy, take one look at the mess and tell the contractor to run, disappear, hide or anything close to that because Trident sure to sue his arse. Well the contractor disappear, and the Grenadian too, and leave the boys hanging on to unemployment.

Now I had a little change save up, so I buy up some rations, store it in my batchy down Newlands and I brace myself for hard times. I enroll in a gym and start pumping iron like a mad man.

1

Now I did done have a big body structure, because my father was a Grenadian (that is how I know the scamps and them can't measure), anyway, in no time at all I start to look like one of them muscle men you does see on them magazines. One day I cruising through Point Fortin, up Frisco junction way, and I see a sign on a door, 'Debt Collector Wanted.' I look at the sign, I look at my muscles and I say to myself, Big John, that sounds like you they looking for boy. When I knock on the door a girl opened it. She looked at me from head to toe in one sweeping glance.

'I want to see the boss-man,' I said.

'Is not a boss-man,' she replied, 'is a boss-lady.'

'Well, whoever hang up that sign outside. I want to see them.'

'Hold on a minute,' the girl said, 'she's interviewing someone right now.'

Well, I holding on and eventually a skinny man came out.

'You can go in now,' said the girl.

I went into the office. It was a small room with a metal desk and a rusty iron chair on one side. On the other side of the desk, in a leather-bound chair, sat a fair-skinned woman with a long nose and a glasses perched at the end of it.

'And your name might be?' she asked.

'John Roberts, but they does call me Big John,' I said. 'I come to check out the work I see advertised on the door.'

'Can you fight?' she asked.

I flexed my upper muscles and asked her, 'What you think?'

She got up, took a pencil off the table, held it at both ends, as if she was going to break it in the middle, and began walking around the room.

'My name is Mrs. Frost. I am a Money Lender.'

She paused, assessing me.

Frowning, she continued, 'Some people are good clients and they pay up on time… others are irresponsible and they renege on their payments,' and, pointing the pencil at me, 'that is where you come in! Whatever methods *you* use to recover *my* money is totally up to you. Out *there*, you are responsible for your actions. Any questions?'

I shook my head.

'You would be paid a percentage of your recoveries and—'

'How much percent?' I cut in.

She bit into her lip. 'Eight percent.'

'Make it ten,' I bargained, 'and you have a debt collector.'

'Ten it is!'

Mrs. Frost and I shook hands.

Then she explained how it would work:

'You would come to me on a Thursday morning and I will give you a list of names, their addresses, photos and the amounts they owe. You begin working there and then. You come back in on a Monday morning with the collections and I pay you your percentage.'

Well, I gone home all excited and I start to devise 'debt collecting' strategies. I open the drawer where I keep my books – now I have to tell you that I am a meticulous fellow; I does document all my goings and comings. The copybook at the top of the drawer mark 'Weekly Expenditures.' I move that aside and dig lower. I come up with one labelled 'Future Plans.' I stash that away. The next one is a new copybook. I take it out and mark 'Debt Collecting Manual' on the cover and I start to make entries. I head up the first page, *Debt Collector's Assets*:

Good manners and to the point.

Physical appearance: flex muscles to look menacing.

Tell of not wanting to use violence.

If violence must be used start slowly.

Always look for signs that client is ready to concede.

Go no further when this is evident.

Next day, I gone in the gym, work out twice as hard, and Thursday morning, bright and early, I in the Boss Lady's office. She hand me a sheet of paper with names, addresses, amounts and photographs stapled to it, and I returned home. I sit down in my batchy, make out a map on a piece of paper and dot in all the addresses I have to check – I have collections to make from Techier to North Trace, Cap-de-Ville. I decide to start in Techier. I get a bottle of Baby Oil, grease down my arms and shoulders until they glowing, and put on an armless jersey and baggy pants; and I hit the road.

I pull up by the first fellar in Techier, call him out, flex my muscles a little and tell him my business. The man gone inside cool-cool and come back with the Boss Lady's money. By midday Saturday I cruising back from North Trace, every name on the list ticked off. I have the Boss Lady's money safe under my mattress: $10,000 in all.

Monday morning, the Boss Lady, smirking, count out my percentage, pass it to me and told me to come back on Thursday for the new list. When I reach in my batchy I count the money again: $1,000. Not bad for a weekend's work. It would have normally take me two weeks to make that much. I smell the money and put it under the mattress.

Well, boy, week after week things going nice. I averaging a $1,000 plus and up to now I ain't even raise my hand as yet. When I walking through the streets of Point Fortin I getting total respect. Sometimes I passing a group of fellars and I hear one saying, 'You see that fellar? Serious debt collecting man, you know! No one messes with him. You see all them muscles? He could rip you to pieces in a minute.' At times like those, I does puff up my chest and walk like Arnold Schwartzanigger.

One Thursday the Boss Lady give me a list with ten names. By Saturday evening I have nine under control. I look at the last address and I see Tanner Street. I say, but that is right close to me, I'll retire now and handle that tomorrow morning. Sunday morning I get up bright and early. I pick up the list and I look at the last picture: was a funny-looking Chinese, with hair that stick up like *pickers* on his head, name Hop Sing. I say, but wait, I don't know no Chinese fellar living on Tanner Street; anyway, I put on my debt collecting clothes, walk over to Tanner Street and continue until I reach the address. I bang on the gate. A funny-looking Chinese fellar come out. He open the gate, bade me come inside and he closed the gate behind me. I said:

'Good morning. I come to collect for the Boss Lady, Mrs. Frost.'

'Oh, so you com' to collect for the Poss Lady. Okay, I com' pack just now.'

He went inside.

A few minutes later he came back dressed up in one of them white karate suits, stood with his legs apart in front me, and just kept looking at me. I say to myself, but what the hell is this, like this Chine'e want to taste my hand or what?

'Where the money?' I asked.

He didn't answer. He just smiled and kept looking at me.

Well, I make to snatch him by his collar but this Chine'e just grab my hand, drop me flat on my back and is kick and karate chop all over my body; and he only bawling, 'hee-hi-haw-yaah!'

I manage to escape.

I stand up.

I say, 'Alright, Sing, you want to play rough! Come!'

Well, who tell me to say that? The man bawl like Bruce Lee and is drop kick straight to chest. I down on the ground again. He make two fingers like a peace sign – I say to myself, oh God he coming for your eyes! Terrified I turn my head just as he was about to strike and his fingers connected with my temple. I blinked. When I pass my hand on my temple I feeling two holes and blood. I say to myself, good move, Big John, if you didn't turn you head he gone with you eyes for sure. Boy, that Chine'e beat me within a inch of my life.

When he realise I was helpless, he bowed and said, 'Y'u better go now, okay,' and he opened the gate.

I drag myself out of there and barely make it home. When I look in the mirror I mash up from head to toe – you would of think a bulldozer pass over me; you would of never believe it was a scrawny little Chinese man that put cutarse on me. I say to myself, I done with this debt collecting shit, tomorrow morning, bright and early, I going to the Boss Lady and tender my resignation.

I start to think a little clearer by evening. I start to reason with myself, 'But how you go leave this work? You making a

5

$1,000 and change a week. It ain't have much Chine'e living in Point, what you worried about?' I start to tax my brain. Eventually I come up with a plan. I will drop in the $9,700 that I already collected and tell the Boss Lady that Hop Sing was not home.

Monday morning, when I went to see the Boss Lady she take a good look at me. 'What happened to you?'

'I went to a party last night, got drunk and fell off a step.'

'That must have been one hell of a long step!' she said.

I gave her the list and the money.

She noticed that the last name was not ticked off. 'And what of Hop Sing?' she asked.

'He wasn't at home,' I lied.

Frowning, she counted out my $970.

I get up vex with myself the next morning. I saying to myself, 'But what the hell wrong with you? You born and grow in Point Fortin, you is the lion in this town and you making some scrawny arse Chinese man from quite China come and run you scared?' I get up from my bed and gone in the kitchen where I had a nice Three Canal cutlass tucked behind the stove. I take it out, walk up to Clifton Hill Beach, swing for Guapo side and walk until I meet the mangrove swamp. I gone in and cut a good piece of mangrove, about three feet long and two inches in diameter. Then I sit down on the beach, peeled off the bark and carved out a sturdy handle, turning it into something like a police baton. All I needed now was something to practise on.

You know what is a *bobolee*? Well a *bobolee* is something that the Point Fortin people does make every Good Friday; is really an effigy of Judas Iscariot. They does construct it out of straw and old rags and then they does dress it up, nice and handsome, with shirt, pants, hat and shoes, and they does scrawl "Judas Iscariot" across its chest. Then they does place it on a street corner and everybody that pass does say, 'Aye look Judas Iscariot, the son-of-a-bitch that betrayed Jesus Christ,' and they does plant some kick and cuff on him right there. By evening they have Judas' body parts scattered all over Point Fortin.

Well I gone home and build a *bobolee*, but instead of marking 'Judas Iscariot,' I mark 'Hop Sing' across his chest, and I gone to work on him with my mangrove baton. In no time at all I have Hop Sing's guts scattered all over my yard. I was ready for anybody.

Thursday morning I gone over by the Boss Lady and collect the list, eight names in all, Hop Sing's name at the bottom of the list. I take out my pen, scratch it off, mark it at the top and I gone home and collect my baton. I say to myself, well Hop Sing, your hour of reckoning is at hand! I step out my batchy feeling confident with my mangrove baton in my hand. I pass Miss Joyce's shop, pass the bus terminal, and nearing the funeral home I meet the undertaker standing on the pavement.

'Morning, Mr. Chad, how business going?' I ask.

'Not good at all, Big John, people hardly dying.'

'Don't worry, Mr Chad, one dead Chine'e coming up in awhile.'

I continue up to the junction, swing right on Tanner Street and walk until I reach Hop Sing's residence. I use my baton to rap on the gate. Hop Sing came out.

'Oh, it's y'u again,' he said, opening the gate.

I stepped inside.

'Yes is me! And I come to collect!'

He looked at my baton. 'So, you com' to collect for the *P*oss Lady. Okay, no ploblem. I go ket it for you.'

Well I stand up there grinning from ear-to-ear and marvelling at the difference my mangrove baton make; I saying to it: 'Boy, like I have to make you a permanent fixture on my debt collecting runs.'

I find Hop Sing taking long and my smile start to narrow. Then I see him coming back, all dressed up in his karate suit. I say, is so! You up to you old trick again? Come with you karate *stupidness*, me and this baton will teach you a little bit of *niggerism*. I have my baton in my right hand, pounding it against my open palm, waiting for him to come.

When he reached about ten feet away he stopped and bowed; when that Chine'e bow I nearly dead! Because he have one of them long Samurai sword strapped to his back. In two-twos he drew it and fly at me. I hear: 'Whatap! Whap! Whap! Whap! Whap!' When I look down I see five pieces of mangrove lying on the ground; I holding a piece about six inches long too. One thing with this negro is he know when to run.

I drop the baton handle and I take off down Tanner Street – I making about ninety; when I reach the corner I chance a look back; the street behind me clear; I take the corner and pass the fire station. When I reach the bank I stop. I watching over the horizon; the coast clear; I double over trying to catch my breath; I feeling weak; my whole body trembling; getting back to my batchy was top priority; but I 'fraid to pass back by Tanner Street, less Hop Sing lurking by the corner waiting to cut me into pieces; I pass around by Hi-Lo, pass the library, pass the court house, down by the old refinery and LNG; don't mind it about four times longer, I not taking chances; when I get home I still trembling, my knees still knocking on their own accord; I say, this is it, I quit, Mrs. Frost have to get a new collector, this shit getting too dangerous; I lie down and trembled off to sleep.

When I get up is almost evening. I feeling a little better so I start to work the brains. I say, look man, you don't have to quit the work, where else you would get a job that paying good money like this? I take up the list – is small money Hop Sing owing. I say to myself, why the hell you don't pay off his debt yourself? Just tick his name off and tomorrow pass around and make the rest of collections. Well, boy, I please with myself. I open the drawer where I had some money stashed away, count out the amount and put it aside. The next day I make the other collections, and Monday morning I take *my own* $500 and pay for that son-of-a-bitch Hop Sing. The Boss Lady check the money ($10,100) and hand me my percentage.

'See you on Thursday,' she said.

When I walking back home, I notice a set of Chinese restaurants opening up all over Point Fortin. What if the Boss Lady sent me to collect from another Chine'e? I get frighten right away. When I get home I begin to pace the floor again. Bam! I hit an idea; I open up the drawer, take out the book marked "Weekly Expenditures" and I make entry:

Chinese Evasion Fund = $25.00

Every week, when I get pay, I religiously putting away $25 in a little box under my bed and I heading up my book. My plan is, if the Boss Lady send me to collect from a Chinese, I ticking off their name one time and paying the money from the fund.

Well, boy, is months now and Mrs. Frost ain't send me to collect from a Chinese, so the fund growing. Right now I have a little chick living in the batchy with me. I sure you did done guess that already because with muscles like mine it was bound to happen; plus, you know them Point girls – them ain't going to leave a man alone for too long that making $1,000 plus a week. Well, we didn't waste time because it look like we have a little one on the way already. Anyway, if I get lucky and the Boss Lady *never* send me to collect from a Chinese, I would have a nice sum stashed away in the Chinese Evasion Fund for my first born when the little fighter comes along. And guess what I going to name him: Hop Sing! Of course.

9

More questions than answers

When I was ten years old my teacher, Mr. Lemessey, gave our class an assignment:

'Walk through the village this weekend and interview three people about the jobs they do. If it's possible, observe them at their work and write a short report of what you see and hear.'

I went home that evening excited by the project. I lived with my Granny and brother, Smithy, who, at twenty, was twice my age. Saturday morning, all keyed up, I armed myself with my copybook and pen and went looking for my first candidate. I walked up the street until I came to the junction. I turned right and walked on until I came to a little parlour.

Mrs. Lakpatia owned the little shop. Her husband, Mr. Lakpatia, had died two years earlier, leaving her with three children. I climbed the two front steps and entered the parlour. It was basically a one room extension at the front of Mrs. Lakpatia's house. The room was divided into two by a counter, the larger side for Mrs. Lakpatia and her goods and the smaller side for customers. From the counter a piece of BRC wire went all the way up to the roof; Mrs. Lakpatia dealt with her customers through a little square cut out of the BRC.

'Good morning, Mrs. Lakpatia,' I said.

'Morning, Andy.'

'I want to do a interview with you.'

'Bout what?' she giggled.

'Bout you and the work that you do.'

She blushed. A child began crying in the house.

'Rooplal, why you don't leave the blasted child alone!' she shouted. 'You want me to come in there and break up you arse? You don't know I answering a interview here!' She turned to me, smiled and, winking, asked, 'So you going to write down everything I say?'

'Everything,' I said.

'Ok, well ask me what you want to know.'

Pen in hand, I opened my copybook. 'What is the name of the job you do?'

'Well… I is a parlour lady. Nah! *Doh* write that! Write I is a proprietor… *ent* that sound more better?'

I wrote:

'*I interviewing Mrs. Lakpatia. She dressed up in a dirty grey dress. She say she is a proprietor and she cursing she children while I interviewing she.*'

'How old is you?' I asked.

'Thirty-three,' she said. She tossed her head back, fixed her hair and, running her palms over her bosom, asked, 'You ain't find I does look younger than that?'

'Yes,' I told her and she smiled—a boy began cursing in the house.

'Ramsingh,' she shouted, 'why you don't hush y'u nasty mouth! You want me to come in there and scrub you tongue with some acid? You just like you blasted father! He couldn't say two words without cussing somebody. That is why he dead like a semp, with he two foot in the air.' She turned to me and smiled. 'So where we was?'

'What is your work about?'

'I does sell to peoples the things they need,' she said. 'I does give them goods and they does give me money.'

I wrote into my copybook.

A child called out from inside the house:

'Ma! Talk to Rooplal! He teasing me!'

'Chandra! Take the *belna* and hit him one on he blasted elbow!' She turned to me. 'Damn children! Can't even do a interview in peace. So where we was?'

I told her that I wanted to observe her while she worked. She agreed. She seemed more excited than me. A few minutes later a woman named Ms Idney came into the shop and asked for a quarter pound of cheese. Mrs. Lakpatia raised a bowl that was on the counter, cut a piece of cheese from a block that was below the bowl, wrapped it in brown paper and placed it on the scale.

'There, quarter pound,' she said, passing the cheese to Ms Idney.

Ms Idney held the cheese in her right hand, moving it up and down, carrying out a weighing process of her own. 'This could never be quarter pound!' she shouted.

'Why you don't hush y'u arse?' Mrs. Lakpatia grumbled.

Ms Idney removed the brown paper and examined the cheese. 'And look,' she said, showing it to me, 'the thing have moss on it!'

'Why the hell you don't go down by Ping and buy you cheese!' Mrs. Lakpatia argued. 'I sure he go give you more than one kind.'

'So you playing wrong and strong?' Ms Idney placed the cheese on the counter. 'Well take back you blasted cheese!' And she stormed out of the parlour.

I wrote all that had happened.

'Never mind that old witch,' she said. 'She always complaining and never have money. So where we was?'

'I still observing,' I said.

'I hope you didn't write what happen there.'

'No I didn't.'

'So who you giving this thing to read when you done write it?'

'My teacher, Mr. Lemessey.'

'You mean the tall, handsome fellar with the curly hair?'

'Yes, that same one.'

'You know how long I watching that man!' she exclaimed.

I closed my copybook.

'Let me see what you write in that book,' she demanded. I knew she would not like what she saw in there, so I clutched the book to my chest.

'Ok-ok... no problem. What you write is your own business... so where we was?'

'I think I finish,' I said.

'Ok, look, I have a sweetie for you.'

She placed the sweetie on her side of the counter and when I reached across she pushed her hand through the opening and grabbed my copybook. Then she sat on a box of condensed milk and began to read.

'But look at my crosses!' she exclaimed. 'You is a real slick one! Who the arse give you permission to write down my conversation with Idney? But look at this little bitch! And you write how I cursing my children too, and you want to carry this for Mr. Lemessey to read! The man that I have my eyes on? Gi'e me y'u pen!'

I handed her my pen. She tore off the page, crumpled it and dropped it to the floor. Then she began to write into my copybook. When she was finished she paused, re-read what she had written, smiled, then she got up and passed my pen and copybook back to me, saying:

'Now take that back to Mr. Lemessey and doh change a word in it, else I make Ramsingh and Rooplal break you arse when you pass by here!'

I took my copybook and pen and hurried off. When I was a good distance from the parlour, I sat in the shade of a coconut tree and opened my copybook. This is what she had written:

'*I interviewing Miss Lakpatia. She dressed up in a clean grey velvet dress, she's a proprietor. She is thirty three years old but she look more like twenty five, she does sell things to peoples and does always give them extras, for example a lady come to buy a piece of cheese and she give the lady one whole ounce extra! She have she place clean and nice and she sheself is very lovely and nice and she speaks nice to she childrens. She husband dead and she lonely for so but she say if she get somebody tall, handsome and educated she won't mind settling again. She gave me a chocolate and tall swee' drink before I go and I want to be a proprietor just like she when I get big.'*

When I was finished reading it, I say to myself, but this not too bad. Plus I dreaded the thought of tangling with Ramsingh and Rooplal at the same time, so I left everything as it was written.

I got up and began to walk towards my home when I met up with Little Mary. She was a stranger that arrived in our village about four months earlier and lived by herself in a hut near the beach.

'Little Mary, I want to interview you,' I say, producing my copybook and pen.

'What! I's a celebrity now! So what you want to interview me about, little man?'

'About you job and thing,' I said.

'Ok, go ahead and ask,' said Little Mary, placing her hands on her hips, and looking down at me clearly amused. 'I listening.'

'What is the name of your job?' I asked.

Little Mary laughed. 'Hmm, I guess you could say that I is a Lady of the Night.'

'How old is you?'

'Eighteen!'

'What you does have to do in your job?'

'I entertains people for a fee.'

'I could observe you while you work?'

'Nah, boy, you mad! You too small for that.'

'But I have to observe you while you work,' I pleaded. 'Else I can't write anything.'

'Nah forget it,' she said and walked away.

A fisherman named Mr. Ombrah was coming up the road the same time.

I ask, 'Mr. Ombrah, what kind of work a Lady of the Night does do?'

'Who tell you about this Lady of the Night business?' he asked.

'Little Mary.'

'Never mind Little Mary and she highfalutin' words,' he said. 'She is nothing more than a damn *jamette*!'

'How you does spell that?' I asked.

He thought about it then said: 'J-A-M-E-T-T-E.'

I wrote it into my copybook while he went his way, then, keeping my distance, I began following Little Mary to see if I could learn anything pertaining to her work.

Little Mary went into her hut, and very soon I noticed men forming a line outside her door. I was puzzled; why would a Lady of the Night have a string of men outside her door in broad daylight? I went and joined the line with the hope of obtaining more information. A fisherman named Tom, who was at the head of the line, began laughing and said: 'What! Like Little Mary entertaining underage customers now!' All the other fishermen in the line began to laugh. The fellar in front, Edmund, turned to me and said: 'I hope she know she have to give you a discount, small man,' and they burst out laughing again.

I noticed that some of the men who went into the hut stayed a long time and some stayed just a couple of minutes. Those who stayed long came out laughing and those who stayed only a couple of minutes came out cursing. When it was almost my turn to get into the hut, I saw my brother, Smithy, coming. He saw me too. He broke a branch from a black sage tree and began peeling the leaves as he came towards me. I didn't expect the first blow.

'What the hell you doing here?' he shouted, and still whipping me, 'You feel you is man now!'

'But what the hell I seeing here, Smithy,' some of the fishermen said. 'You don't have to lash the boy. Is you alone like sweetness?' And everyone laughed.

Embarrassed, I ran off clutching my copybook and pen, and when I looked back I saw that Smithy had joined the line. When I reached home I wrote into my copybook:

'*I interviewing Little Mary. She say she work as a Lady of the Night, but Mr. Ombrah tell me she nothing more than a damn jamette! I find it strange that although she tell me she is a Lady of the Night, she have a long*

15

line of men outside she door in broad daylight. She does make she money by either making these men laugh or curse.'

When I was finished I closed my copybook, tucked it under my arm and went off to interview the overseer on the coconut estate. I interviewed him, wrote the details and thought all was well.

Monday morning Mr. Lemessey picked up all the books and placed them on his table. Then he started going through them one-by-one, every now and then stopping to read a piece to the class that caught his fancy. Eventually he picked up my book (I knew it was my copybook because of the dog ears in the corner; my copybooks always had dog ears). He read the first part that was written by Mrs. Lakpatia to the class.

'Very good, Andy,' he said, nodding, then he went all quiet, and stopped nodding, and he started to get red, and I started to get frighten because when Mr. Lemessey get vex he does get red. He shouted, 'Anderson! Bring your tail up here!'

I knew something was wrong, but couldn't figure what so I walked slowly. When I reached his desk he grabbed me.

'Anderson! You... you perverted little bitch! This is the kind of nastiness you writing in the government copy book!'

The class began to giggle when Mr. Lemessey snatched a tamarind whip from the desk, made me bend over and clench my pants at the buttocks, and gave me a sound licking. I went back to my seat, more confused than hurt, but it did not end there.

One month later, my confusion deepened when I was entering Granny's bedroom. I stopped when I heard Smithy say:

'Granny, I going to get married.'

Granny, in a slow and weary voice, asked, 'To who Smithy?'

'To *Mary*.'

Granny sounded confused: '*Mary*? Who is that?'

Smithy whispered, 'You know nah, Granny, Little Mary.'

'Holy Moses, Smithy! Like you gets you head all mixed up, son.'

There was some silence so I entered the room. Smithy said:

'Listen, boy, you don't see two big people having a conversation? March you tail out of here right now!'

I walked heavily against the wooden floor so that they could hear me going to the gallery, then I stopped, tiptoed back and put my ears against the wall.

Smithy sounded upset. 'What you mean I all mixed up?'

'Son, when a man is ready to takes a wife, he looks for a girl with special qualities, a girl that he knows belongs only to himself. Not a raffle where every other man takes a chance or a *sou-sou* where every man takes a hand. Bless your soul, child, try and see the light.'

'Granny, you not listening. Sit down and let me tell you something,' said Smithy; the bed creaked under Granny's weight. 'You remember last week Saturday I didn't come home at all?'

'And the Saturday befores that too,' Granny added.

'Well, Saturday night I went and take a little gamble with the boys down on the beach–'

'But, Smithy,' Granny cut in, 'I tolds you that gambling is an abomination to the Lord.'

'I know, but hear me out Granny. The *wappie* was going nice, I winning the boys a lot of money. Little Mary come and place her arms around me while I was playing–'

'So that is the kinds of idolatry you does be up to on a Saturdays night?' Granny asked, her voice growing angry.

'Just hear me out, Granny,' Smithy pleaded. 'She placed her arms around me and whispered in my ear, "Give me some of that money let me buy something for we to drink." I gave her five dollars and she came back with two beers. This continued until my head started to get bad. So I say to the boys, I quit, and then Little Mary whispered, "You going home with me tonight, young boy–"'

Suddenly Smithy shouted, 'Andy! That is you out there listening, you *macocious* little bitch?'

I had removed a crown cork from my pocket and was scratching the wall subconsciously.

Smithy shouted, 'I coming out there to deal with you!'

Quickly, I placed the cork into my pocket, tiptoed to the gallery and sat unconcerned. When he entered the gallery he seemed puzzled.

'Oh, I thought you was over by the wall there listening.'

'You always blaming me for something I didn't do,' I said, looking hurt.

He twisted his mouth and went back inside. I tiptoed back to my position just in time to hear him ask:

'Whe' we reach, Gran'?'

Granny scolded him for addressing me rudely and said, 'You reach where Little Mary asks you to go home with her.'

'Right, we leave the gamble and going home by Little Mary. In my pocket I have about two hundred and fifty dollars in winnings. When we get there Little Mary take out a bottle of rum and encourage me to drink. I take a few drinks and then I knock out cold. Sometime during the night Little Mary get up and steal all the money from my pants pocket.'

'And you wants to marry a girl like that?' Granny wondered.

'I ain't finish,' Smithy said impatiently.

Granny apologised.

'When I get up in the morning, I see Little Mary standing over me, tears running down her face. I asked her what was wrong. She did not answer but continued crying so I asked her again. She told me that she had stolen my money and she reached under the mattress, came out with the money and give it back to me. She said she was really sorry, how she was fed up and unhappy with the life she was leading. I feel sorry for she and told her to keep the money but she would not accept it. I put the money in my pocket, tried to console her and left. That was Sunday morning. I hear, when the boys went over to patronise her, she locked up her hut tight and wouldn't let any of them in. The boys keep going back day after day but no response from Little Mary. I decides to check her out the Thursday and guess what? When she heard my voice she opened the door for me. We talked for a while. She told me she was finished with that type of life. She wants to get a job, go to church and settle down.'

'Well bless my soul, Hallelujah, Praise the Lord!' Granny exclaimed. 'Oh dear me... continue, sonny boy.'

'Well, I going back every day after that and talking to her. And guess what?'

'What?'

'I fall smack in love with her,' he confessed. 'This morning I asked her to marry me.'

Granny's voice deepened: 'And?'

'And she agreed!'

'You not worried what peoples would think and say?' Granny asked.

Smithy's voice was firm: 'He that is without sin cast the first stone.'

'Smithy, I's mighty proud of you, son. *Today* I knows that I've raised you proper. Glory be to The Most High! Come gives your Granny a hug, boy... I so proud of you! I will speak to the priest tomorrow.'

One month later Smithy and Little Mary got married in the village church. Smithy rented a hut right on our street, and Granny and I were left alone. Every time I passed in front of Smithy's hut I looked to see if there was a line of fellars waiting to get in, but there never was. Sometimes Little Mary would call me and give me sweets that she made. On one of these occasions I asked her:

'Little Mary, you does still work as a Lady of the Night?'

Smithy was writing a note at the table. 'Who you calling Little Mary?' He grabbed a broom stick and rushed to hit me, saying, 'My wife's name is *Mary*!'

Mary restrained him. 'Is alright, Smithy, he is only a little boy.' She turned to me. 'No Andy, I am now the wife of Smithy and I no longer does that type of work.' She turned to my brother. 'Smithy, please... go and finish what you was doing.'

Smithy glared at me and returned to his writing.

Mary smiled. 'Now hurry along and remember to share your sweets with Granny.'

After a few months, the man that rented the hut to Smithy raised the rent. Granny convinced Smithy and *Mary* to move in with us (a carpenter came and added a room to our house). *Mary* was always busy, cooking, cleaning, washing and fussing over Smi-

19

thy, Granny and me. *Mary* began making sugarcakes, fudge and touloum, and I went around the village selling them for her.

One Sunday morning, Granny, *Mary* and I were going to church. A group of fishermen were standing in front Mr. Ping's shop. Fisherman Tom called out:

'Eh-eh! Little Mary! You going to church now! Like you want to c-o-r-r-u-p-t the priest and all?'

All the fishermen laughed; I saw panic in *Mary's* face.

Granny took her hand, squeezed it and, leading her on, said, 'Never mind him, *Mary*, is only the devil's imp trying to be noticed.'

One year after *Mary* and Smithy moved in, she made a baby boy, and our house was filled with joy. *Mary* was a good housewife, taking care of her family and still finding time to make her sweets. She never missed church on a Sunday. She had turned around our lives: there were flowers blooming in pots on the banister around the gallery, the kitchen always had an inviting smell, and Granny looked younger than when she lived alone with Smithy and I. One Saturday Granny's sister, Aunt Silla, came to spend the weekend. That night, me lying between the two old ladies, Granny said:

'Bless my heart, Silla, but it's funny how some things that happened two thousand years ago could happens again in our lifetime.'

'What you talking 'bout?' snapped a sleepy Aunt Silla.

'Why, the woman at the well with Jesus.'

'What woman at which well?' Aunty Silla yawned.

'The woman at the well in Samaria. The one who confessed her sins to Jesus and turned around her life.'

'And what of that?' asked Aunt Silla.

'It's the exact story with Smithy's wife, our own *Mary*.'

No response. Granny dozed off too, and they began snoring like only old ladies could snore. I lay there between them, unable to sleep but thinking, Lady of the Night or lady at the well? It didn't make much sense to me. All I knew was that I loved my sister-in-law, Little Mary; I loved *Mary* a lot.

Franklyn the Lagahoo

Manuel Lacouray was a jovial little man with a magnificent bald-head that dazzled villagers when the sun was out. He took great pride in this fact too and whenever someone asked if he rubbed his head with tallow grease or, perhaps, coconut oil, he would sadden and say:

'But why it is you all can't understand that is a natural shine? I ain't put *nothing* on it. I never rub anything on it. The Lord know that I is a good man, so he put that light to shine on my head for others to see.'

And it was true. Manuel Lacouray was a good man. He would rise with the sun, pick the ripened fruits from his trees and go through the village, sharing them with the little children before they filtered off to school. Manuel's house stood just off the main road at the end of a narrow track. The house itself was small but his yard was very large and he kept it spotlessly clean. During the week he spent most of his time on his knees, pulling specks of grass and weeds that tried to disturb the creamy-white sand. Manuel had neither wife nor child but on Fridays he raked the entire yard in preparation for the weekend, when all the village children would come to play there.

When the children played Manuel became a commentator. He would hold a dried coconut shell to his mouth, like a micro-phone, and commentate as if he worked for a radio station. If cricket was in season they played cricket, and Manuel would give the children famous names like Hunte, Sobers and Kanhai. After the game he shared out prizes, giving the best fruits to the child who scored the most runs and the one who took the most wickets; he shared the rest equally among the other children. When football was in season they played football and he did pretty much the same thing. With Manuel everyone was a winner.

When Manuel Lacouray died suddenly, the entire village plunged into deep mourning.

Two weeks after his death, Manuel's house was occupied by his brother, Franklyn, who came from a "distant village." Franklyn was the opposite of Manuel, both in stature and ways. He was a tall, dark man with lily-white teeth that appeared even whiter than snow because of a gold splice tucked between his upper front teeth. He had a full head of grey-black hair. The villagers noticed the difference between Manuel and Franklyn the moment he arrived in the village.

As he came off the bus a brown suitcase he was carrying fell and opened, spilling his belongings onto the road—Edward Joseph, who was standing nearby, rushed over to help him. Franklyn pushed him away. But Edward noticed the book. It was a black book with a red cross and a dragon's head above the cross. When Edward went around telling the villagers about it they all said that it was a bad book. Franklyn never spoke to the villagers and rarely even smiled, but when he did, it was more of a provocative grin than a smile.

A few months after Franklyn's arrival villagers began reporting sightings of unusual animal behaviour. Seulal James, walking on a moonlit night, saw a boar pig standing on its hind legs and pissing against a coconut tree. Villagers told spooky stories of chains jangling around their houses at night, only to look out and see a large "hog cattle" walking away. One night, Venora Hart, a very beautiful woman whom Franklyn usually stared at in a penetrating way, heard barking outside her gate. When she went out she saw a large, black dog standing there. The dog growled: 'I come to spend the night with you.' Screaming, Venora rushed back inside and locked herself away. She would forever swear that she saw a gold splice in the dog's mouth.

Fingers of suspicion began wagging in Franklyn's direction. Some villagers said that he could never be Manuel Lacouray's brother. They said he was an imposter, an evil shape shifter, who had come to steal Manuel's property; and it grieved them that Manuel's beautiful yard was no more. Bush and vines had grown over it, right up to the sides of the house, and threatened to get onto the roof. When children were going to school, they crossed the road when passing the house. The mysterious sightings in the village increased. No one ventured out at night. No one, except Zambie Coot.

Zambie Coot, twenty three, big-mouthed and rambunctious, lived with his mother in a tiny house, with a long verandah joining it to a smaller building which served as a kitchen; the structures sat on shortish wooden stilts. In the kitchen there was a crude bed. Zambie slept in there. Zambie's mother, Ma Coot, was a small, frail, bent woman of sixty. She was a staunch Catholic from birth who never missed mass on a Sunday. It was said that she knew more prayers than the pope himself and had such faith that she could move Mt El Tucuche all alone by her frail little self. Zambie Coot loved the cinema and he said that no stranger playing Lagahoo would frighten him from the late movies at least once or twice a week. In fact, he said, he was going to put a good cutarse on Franklyn as soon as he found the time.

One Sunday morning Zambie Coot got his chance. Around this era, everyone used outhouses, always built some distance from the living quarters. It was acceptable for someone walking on the road, and getting an urgent intestinal call, to run into the closest outhouse even if it wasn't theirs. Franklyn was out walking when he got a "hot one." He dashed for the Coots' outhouse. Zambie, sitting on the verandah, saw him and smiled wickedly. He jogged down the steps, crawled under the house and dragged out a basket of empty bottles. He waited until he thought Franklyn was thoroughly occupied. Then he began shelling the outhouse with bottles. A terrified Franklyn scrambled out, still pulling up his pants,

23

and bolted away, with Zambie in hot pursuit, armed with a few bottles, still pelting at Franklyn until he had no more.

The next night the Tivoli cinema in Cedros was showing *Shenandoah*, starring James Stewart, and Zambie never missed a James Stewart movie. He got ready early and walked to the seven o'clock show.

Just after midnight, under a brilliant full moon, a sleepy Zambie was making his way along the path that led to his home. When he was within one hundred yards of the house he passed a large "hog cattle," and the "hog cattle" said:

'You know how long I waiting for you?'

Maybe it was because of the sleepiness but, somehow, Zambie didn't catch on. But he was sure he had heard someone say something. When he looked over his shoulder the "hog cattle" smiled; there was no mistaking those lily white teeth and the glowing gold splice. Zambie took off like a jet: into his yard, up the steps, across the verandah and into the kitchen. The "hog cattle" didn't give up. It raced into the yard and began butting the kitchen with its large horns.

Ma Coot, hearing the commotion, opened her window and saw the "hog cattle" in all its fury. 'Oh, is Franklyn come to practise his *negromancy*. Well he come to the wrong place tonight!'

Quietly, she swooped up her rosary and a bottle of holy water, opened the door, crossed the verandah and entered the kitchen. Zambie was in a corner trembling like a leaf. Mat Coot whispered:

'Listen, son, no matter what happen in here tonight, you not to utter a word. If you only talk he would get away. I have him right where I want him and I will keep him here until daylight. Let the whole village come in the morning and see that Franklyn is the man that turning beast in the night.'

And with her rosary in hand, Ma Coot opened the kitchen window and began raining down prayers on the "hog cattle," every now and then sprinkling it with holy water; the beast froze. Now Ma Coot was on her knees, her chin resting on the window sill, the rosary dangling outside the open window. She was in constant prayer. Around two o'clock she stunned the "hog cattle" with a

24

repertoire of *Hail-Marys*, *Act of Contrition* and the *Magnificat*. The "hog cattle" began to froth; the kitchen became hot like an oven; yet Zambie still trembled in one corner. Around four in the morning the "hog cattle" began tapping some of its own powers; the kitchen shook—plates, condiments, bottles and other small objects trembled off the kitchen shelves and shattered at Zambie Coot's feet. He wanted to scream, but he remembered Ma Coot's warning to not speak. Five o'clock, daylight wasn't too far now, Ma Coot pierced the "hog cattle" with some of her most powerful verses. The "hog cattle," sensing sunrise, summoned the last of its powers. The beast breathed fire from its nostrils; the kitchen became hot like a furnace and shook like it would collapse. Zambie bawled, "I can't take it no more, Ma! Untie the beast!" The spell broke. Ma Coot fell on her face and pounded the kitchen floor in frustration, while the "hog cattle" wobbled away.

That very morning Franklyn packed up his belongings and left Icacos by bus.

The next day the villagers burnt Manuel Lacouray's house to the ground.

Mendoza's gold

Across The Serpent's Mouth from *Icacos Village* lies the *Venezuelan mainland*. Between these two land masses is an island called *Soldado Rock*. From Soldado Rock a huge reef stretches southward. West of Soldado Rock, on the Venezuelan mainland, is the *Pedernales River*. One mile up this river sits a sleepy little village called *Capure*. Another half mile up the river is *Pedernales*, larger but just as sleepy. In 1929 winds of change blew through these villages, awakening inhabitants. A U.S. survey company discovered large petroleum deposits in and around both villages. The Americans moved quickly to harvest the oil. Infrastructure had to be put in place and labour was in great demand. The company issued a tender in the villages for someone to supply them with labour. Tenders came in from prominent persons in both villages but everyone believed someone from Pedernales would win the bid, since more influential persons lived there.

Lo and behold, Mr. Mendoza from Capure won the contract. Some said it was because he spoke English, but many whispered 'voodoo'. Mendoza was a tall, slim, mysterious man. Those who knew him well said his temper lay at the end of a very short fuse. Mendoza owned a fleet of small fishing boats. Once, one of his fishing boats rescued a Trinidadian fisherman floating on wreckage. They brought him to Capure and Mendoza took him in. He lived with Mendoza for almost two years. During this time

Mendoza learned a little English. One day the Trinidadian disappeared. Some said the night of his disappearance there was a bitter argument between the two. The Trinidadian was never seen again.

Mendoza moved swiftly and assembled his labour force, hiring men from both villages. The project was off to a quick start but it was going to be a long haul. The contract stated Mendoza would pay his employees weekly, and every two months the company would pay him. The Americans had an office in Caracas, Venezuela, hundreds of miles from Capure, but they also had an office in Port of Spain, Trinidad, about seventy miles from Capure. Mr. Mendoza negotiated to collect the money in Trinidad and the company made the arrangements. The company paid in solid gold, American golden eagle coins to be exact; the acceptable world currency in those days. The gold came from America, onboard an airplane that brought mail to Trinidad, and was stored at the company's Port of Spain office.

Because Mendoza's fishing boats were small, he rented *The Cordoba* for the voyages to Port of Spain, where he collected his strongbox of gold. *The Cordoba* belonged to a Mr. Ayala who rented it at a steep price. After a few trips Mr. Mendoza, whose profits were soaring, offered a lucrative sum for the boat. Mr. Ayala decided to sell and the deal was clinched.

The boat, a thirty-one-foot Margaritian-built vessel, with a tiny, three-cylinder engine, gave up to eight knots in a following sea. It was basically an open boat with a little roof covering the stern. Immediately upon purchasing the vessel, Mendoza sent his brother-in-law, Hernandez Olario, his right-hand man, with the boat to the dockyard in Guiria, a port about thirty miles north-northeast of Capure. There they refurbished *The Cordoba* and gave it a new coat of white paint.

The Cordoba returned to Capure and there was a large celebration in its honor. It was marvelous to see the refurbished, Margaritian-built craft with its glistening white coat steaming towards Capure. When they moored *The Cordoba* alongside the wooden jetty in Capure, Mr. Mendoza broke the traditional bottle of champagne against the bow and the celebrations began.

In Icacos Village, Trinidad, thirteen miles from Capure as the crow flies, while the festivities in honour of *The Cordoba* were heating up, an Indian man, Chaitram, a direct descendant of indentured labourers, was chopping away at a bamboo clump with his cutlass. Chaitram worked tirelessly, hacking away at the skinny bamboo stalks on the outside so he could get to the fat ones in the middle. Chaitram stopped. He flicked sweat from his brow with his right index finger then with the thumb of the same hand tested his blade's edge. Mumbling, he took out a file from his back pocket, leaned against one of the stouter bamboo stalks, spat on the blade and began sharpening it. He tested the blade again, smiled and attacked the larger stalks. He chopped with his right hand, while his left fanned away mosquitoes circling his face. The sun shone overhead and Chaitram's ragged old shirt clung to his wet body. He cursed the humidity and mosquitoes working in tandem to discourage his efforts. But Chaitram, who had already done his 'task' on the Constance Coconut Estate during the wee hours of the morning, worked without pause. Slowly but deliberately he felled bamboo.

When his right hand was tired he stopped chopping and dragged the felled stalks away from the clump. One by one he got them out and stacked them. After he picked up his calabash gourd and pulled the plug. He sipped, savouring the water, and then raised the gourd over his head, tilting it, allowing water to run onto his hair and face, then he shook his head, violently, scattering water droplets. Refreshed, Chaitram smiled. He placed the gourd on the ground, held the bottom of his shirt in both hands and wiped his face. He sighed contentedly and counted the stalks, twenty six in all; nine less than he had in mind. He would return tomorrow.

The day after the celebrations in Capure, Mr. Mendoza and his brother-in-law, Hernandez Olario, took *The Cordoba* three miles upriver where, in the middle of nowhere, lived his aunt, an old woman known only as La Bruha. There were conflicting reports on La Bruha. Some said she was spiritual, others that she dealt in the occult. She lived all alone on the river bank, in a little clearing that only the people who did business with her ventured into. It was widely believed she was responsible for Mendoza winning the contract. When they got to the clearing they anchored *The Cordoba*, put a skiff into the water and went ashore.

La Bruha was expecting her visitors. She was a frail woman, bent at the back and walked with a stick. La Bruha wore a black lace scarf and her lips appeared a brilliant red. She shuffled around the claustrophobic hut serving coffee. While they drank, she placed vials of colourful liquids into an old wicker basket. When the men finished their coffee, she took them into the clearing and showed them a black fowl cock with a large, red comb.

The men stood staring at the cock. La Bruha motioned that they should catch it. They began to chase the cock, but it was quick and the clearing was muddy and they fell whenever the cock changed directions. La Bruha emitted a strange noise and thrust out her walking stick. The cock flew into the air and landed on the stick, and La Bruha grabbed its legs with her left hand. The cock flapped its wings furiously, trying to break free but La Bruha's gnarled hand held it firm. She looked at Mendoza and laughed: a throaty sound that scared Olario. She beckoned to Olario, gave him the cock and she and Mendoza returned to the hut. La Bruha pointed to a golden sword hanging on the wall and told Mendoza to retrieve it. With the stick in her left hand, she cradled the wicker basket with the vials and the trio walked to the river bank. The men lifted La Bruha into the skiff and rowed to *The Cordoba*.

It took some time to get La Bruha onto *The Cordoba* but once aboard, she went about her business. The atmosphere around *The Cordoba* was quite noisy, with numerous birds whistling in the sunshine and baboons howling in their early morning play. La Bruha held up her stick and let out another strange throaty noise; an eerie silence descended on the area. She sprinkled her vials of colourful liquids throughout *The Cordoba*. An uncomfortable Olario lowered his gaze whenever La Bruha turned his way. She took the sword from Mendoza and shuffled to the bow. Olario gaped in astonishment when the old witch squatted and pissed on the sword.

La Bruha motioned for the cock and Mendoza, sensing Olario's unwillingness, fetched the feathered sacrifice. La Bruha gave him the sword. Pinching the magnificent red comb, Mendoza pinned the transfixed fowl against the bow and, with a vicious swing of the golden sword, chopped off its head. The head bounced around the bow while Mendoza held the cock's body, blood gushing out the bobbing neck, sprinkling the area around him. The head plopped into the river, spreading a red circle where it entered. Olario, watching from the centre of the boat, felt sick. He knelt at *The Cordoba's* gunwale and vomitted into the river.

Across the waters of The Serpent's Mouth, Chaitram had finished his 'task' on the coconut estate and was on his way to the bamboo clump, east of the estate. Armed with his cutlass, calabash gourd, file and a bit of string, he walked purposely towards his destination. On arrival he sharpened his cutlass and attacked his task with gusto. He chopped until he had the deficit nine stalks.

Chaitram sat on the sand, leaned against an old coconut tree stump and reflected on his life. He was unhappy with his lot. The money he earned on the estate wasn't enough to put food on the table. He saw the frightening results on his three sons: their skin sagged from their bones with little or no flesh in between. He had to do something. This *thing* he was going to build was on his mind a long time, but long work hours had prevented him. So, he had spoken to the estate manager and asked to work 'task'. The manager had agreed. 'Task' meant he began work at four in the morning and stopped by ten, so he had the rest of the day to do as he pleased. He had told his wife, Dularie, about *it* and she agreed *it* was good. Then he relayed *it* to his cousin, Padam, who also worked 'task' and he agreed to get the roll of wire they needed. Padam also said he'd join the project as soon as Chaitram was finished cutting the bamboo. Chaitram was confident when this *thing* was completed he would be able to put *real* food on the table.

Chaitram stood from his reverie, took a long drink from his gourd and extracted the string from his pocket. The string was fourteen feet long; he knew this because he had measured it against one of the coconut carts. Sebastien, the man in charge of the estate workshop, had confirmed the cart was fourteen feet long. Chaitram wanted *it* to be the length of the cart. Chaitram knelt beside a fallen bamboo stalk, licked the tip of his index finger, held one end of the string and rolled it until twisty. He tied the end of the string to the fatter end then, creeping on his knees, he traced the string along the length of the bamboo. At the end of the string, he took the cutlass and marked the spot. He loosened the string, rolled it into a tiny ball and pocketed it. He chopped off the excess from the stalk and used this piece as a template to measure the rest. One by one he trimmed the other eight pieces. With the file, he sharpened his blade and attacked the twenty six pieces of the day before.

The sun leaned way over to the west as Chaitram trudged home. Dularie saw him coming and immediately stoked the fireside to heat up his dhal and rice and coconut chutney. His three sons stood outside the barrack house waiting to greet him. They looked skinny and malnourished, with their big, bulging eyes and ever-present gobs of golden snot in their nostrils. They'd get fat and round like suckling pigs, thought Chaitram, as soon as he finished building *it*. As he neared them, he lifted his cutlass and lurched as if to chase them. They giggled and raced up the three steps into the tiny gallery. Dularie stood, hands on hips, smiling at the gaming of her four, the fireside flickering precariously close to her ragged dress.

'Yuh work-am late today, man,' she said.

'Yes, gyal, me *finish* cut-am all de bamboo.'

Dularie smiled again and her premature wrinkles, induced by life's hardship, disappeared when Chaitram nodded at her appro-vingly. He placed his cutlass and gourd on the bottom step and sat on the middle step. The boys ran back down, the younger ones quickly claiming places on his lap. Balgobin, the eldest, sat beside him and embraced his father's shoulder. Chaitram turned to Balgo-bin, placed his left arm around the boy's neck and using the thumb and index finger of his right hand, squeezed the boy's nose, releas-ing a chunk of snot. He whipped his hand and the snot landed on the sand. A common fowl raced over and swallowed the phlegm.

Chaitram repeated the process on the younger boys, each time the fowl claiming its prize. He reached for the gourd, pulled the plug and gave the gourd to Balgobin who poured water on his father's hands. Dularie brought her husband's food in half of a calabash gourd fashioned into an eating utensil. Chaitram used his fingertips to mix the dhal, rice and coconut chutney. He scooped a bit of the mixture into his youngest son's mouth, did the same with Balgobin and the other boy then he began to feed himself.

'Mmm taste-am good, gyal,' he said, between mouthfuls, and Dularie smiled.

'Me put-am geera in de dhal and bhandania in de coconut chutney,' she said happily.

'Yes, gyal, me *like-am* de chutney,' Chaitram winked.

'You *like-am* de chutney? Well tonight me *give-am* yu chutney wit plenty pepper befo yu sleep.'

Chaitram smiled, winked and swallowed the last mouthful. He wiped the inside of the makeshift bowl, coming away with a residue of rice and dhal on his forefinger which he sucked, sensuously then he sighed contentedly.

The Cordoba was due to sail to Port of Spain in one week, but Mr. Mendoza had a problem. Hernandez Olario, his right-hand man and brother-in-law, had deserted him. Mendoza could not figure why Olario quit and had tried to lure him back with higher wages, but Olario had packed his bags and left on a boat bound for Guiria. Mendoza knew Olario was a hard man to replace: he was trustworthy, a good captain and handy with a shotgun.

During the time Mendoza had rented *The Cordoba*, he used a three-man crew: his second cousin Juan Pablo, Hernandez Olario and himself. During these voyages Mendoza left his wife and seventeen-year-old son, Jimenez, in charge of the labour contract. With Olario gone he had to restructure things. Pablo was just as good a captain as Hernandez. He would make Pablo captain, and go along himself. Because he did not trust outsiders, he would draft Jimenez. It was a good crew, Mendoza thought, but he would have to keep an eye on Pablo and his drinking habit. Settled on his crew,

Mendoza relaxed, knowing he had a few days to make adjustments, if necessary.

Chaitram headed towards the bamboo clump for the third time. Today three men walked behind him. He had invited his cousin, Padam, to join the project, but Padam had taken it upon himself to invite Manbode and Rambir. Chaitram walked with heaviness because he did not trust Manbode and Rambir. Both were greedy and he distrusted the way Manbode always walked around with his cutlass strapped to his waist as if it were a third arm. Chaitram pulled Padam aside.

'Why yu bring-am these two greedy goondas fo?'

Padam explained the only way he could have sourced the roll of binding wire and pliers was through Manbode, since he worked in the estate workshop; Manbode had insisted he bring along Rambir. The arrangement displeased Chaitram, but eight hands were better than four.

When they got to the bamboo clump Chaitram explained what he wanted. They placed the wire and pliers on the root of a coconut tree and dragged the bamboo stalks down to the seashore. They lined them up alongside each other and Padam brought the instruments and began snipping the wire. Armed with a fistful of wire each man began fastening the bamboo stalks together. They worked silently, creeping on their knees like babies in the sand as they moved to and fro, measuring here and strapping there until they had fashioned a *raft*.

The men looked at their craft then at each other and smiled. They eased it along the sand, past the tiny breaking of waves and into the placid sea. The raft floated like a ship. The men sat on the structure and paddled around with their hands, splashing water on each other and laughing like little boys.

'Eh, eh, raft float-am like Tetanic!' shouted Padam gleefully.

'Wha is Tetanic?' asked Rambir.

'Eh you *gadahar*,' said Padam, 'you nah know wha Tetanic is? Tetanic is big arse ship that hit-am ice bag and sink-am in sea near D'merica.'

Manbode looked at Padam and scoffed, 'Is nah Tetanic, is Tatianic.'

The two men argued at length while Chaitram and Rambir laughed. Padam won the argument so Chaitram christened the raft *Tetanic*. Sulking, Manbode shifted to the starboard side, his feet dangling in the water.

They floated around for a while then, carefully, dragged the *Tetanic* up the sloping shore and concealed it with dried coconut branches. They went into the nearby swamp where they cut four stout pieces of mangrove. Back on the beach, each man sculpted a paddle with their cutlass. They hid the paddles under the dried branches concealing the *Tetanic*.

That evening the four men went to Baban's little shop located at the edge of the estate settlement and purchased hooks and strings. That night, under flambeaux light and with boyish excitement, they constructed fishing lines, using discarded nuts and bolts as sinkers.

Next morning, just after ten o'clock, the four men hustled to the *Tetanic*, each armed with his fishing gear. Chaitram shouldered a length of rope rolled in small circles; he had found this on the beach days before and saved it for an anchor rope. Manbode carried a stainless steel shaft with iron prongs tied to it; this would be their anchor. He had spent most of his morning's working hours fashioning it in the estate's workshop, while Sebastien turned a blind eye because Manbode had promised him the first fish he caught. Rambir held the bait: a can of salted herrings he got from a fisherman. They hustled along excitedly.

At the beach they removed the branches, retrieved their paddles and launched the *Tetanic*. Their equipment on board, Chaitram secured the rope to the anchor and they paddled out to sea. At first the raft made S's in the water, but as the men developed a rhythm the *Tetanic* moved in a straight line. Quarter mile offshore Chaitram held up his paddle; the others stopped. Padam dropped anchor. Skillfully, they baited their lines and threw them into the water.

Manbode drew first blood: a red snapper about three pounds. The men shouted in glee as Manbode unhooked it from his line and threw it in the middle of the *Tetanic*, and they looked on in awe as the lovely redfish flipped about in its death throes. One by one the others got into the act as fishes went after their bait. They caught snappers, cavalis and grunts. The excitement was infectious; they competed against each other, pulling in fish until there was hardly room to sit. They pulled in the anchor and headed to shore, singing in Hindi as they paddled, the little raft laden with fish. On shore they offloaded the catch and secured the raft. Manbode elected himself divider, distributing the fish into four heaps with the big ones going into his.

'Eh-eh, Manbode, yu take-am all big fish for self and give-am all small fish to we,' said Chaitram, stopping the sharing process.

Manbode huffed, 'But me ketch-am most big one.'

Annoyed, Chaitram restored the fish into one heap and allowed each man to alternately choose. When the main heap was the size of each man's, Chaitram stopped them.

'And who tha pile fo?' inquired Manbode.

'Fo other poor peoples in de estate,' said Chaitram.

Manbode *steupsed* and spat on the sand.

The Cordoba sailed out of Capure on a Sunday afternoon bound for Port of Spain with a family crew onboard and an American passenger hitching a ride. Despite calm weather a strong current ran against them so they had a smooth, snail-like crossing. They reached the Port of Spain harbor in the wee hours of Monday and anchored *The Cordoba* off the mangrove.

At first light they lowered the skiff and Mendoza, his son Jimenez, and the American went ashore. The American bought them breakfast at a café and after eating went his way. Mendoza took the boy to the company's office. He arranged to pick up the gold at three o'clock that afternoon. He then toured the city with Jimenez and purchased a few things. Following an early lunch they rowed back to *The Cordoba*. Mendoza allowed Captain Pablo an

35

hour ashore. Pablo, a small wiry man who from a distance looked more like a boy, zipped for a familiar rumshop on the waterfront. Pablo gulped down a nip of Trinidad's strongest rum and purchased another, concealing it cleverly in his jacket. He rowed back to *The Cordoba*. At two o'clock Mendoza and Jimenez left *The Cordoba* again and by four-thirty they had the strongbox containing the gold safely on board. At five o'clock they weighed in the anchor.

The Northeast Trades blew gently as *The Cordoba* eased its way out of the Port of Spain harbor. The sun was already dipping close to the western horizon. Captain Pablo, at the tiller, shaded his eyes against the lowering sun and coaxed *The Cordoba* west-southwesterly. The sun traded its yellow sheen for lava red as it slipped behind the far off sea. Mendoza and Jimenez stood forward, the father pointing out and naming the silhouetted islands in the Grand Bocas.

Mendoza extracted a hurricane lantern from a wooden box. He knelt in the bottom of the boat, scratched a match, lifted the shade of the lantern and held the flame to the wick; the wick caught, flickered and then the flame was constant. Mendoza lowered the shade and secured the lantern on a hook in the middle of the boat.

Two hours out of Port of Spain the Northeast Trades exchanged its gentle breeze for a more prominent wind speed. *The Cordoba* rolled restlessly as she chugged along into the darkness. Steadily, the wind speed increased, until it whistled through the woodwork of *The Cordoba*. Then, this whistling demon unleashed its fury on the Gulf of Paria, churning the normally placid water into angry, dreadful waves. *The Cordoba* dipped and rolled dangerously but gallantly ploughed on. The waves came in a brutal, organised pattern from the northeast. *The Cordoba* was taking a fearsome beating on her starboard stern. While water splashed over the gunwale and into the boat, Mendoza and Jimenez feverishly worked the hand pump.

Captain Pablo knew they were in for a long night. Satisfied that Mendoza and son were occupied, he held the tiller with his left hand, dipped into his pocket with the other and clutched his nip of consolation. He removed the cover, gulped a mouthful of rum and pocketed the bottle. Pablo spat into the water and, now, with two hands on the tiller, he fought to hold *The Cordoba* against the raging elements. One minute she raced down a wave, the next she sat in a valley between two, seemingly lost, then, slowly, she would rise to the crest of another monster.

Mendoza looked at his son in the lantern's glare. The boy showed no sign of sea sickness as he worked the hand pump. It was a good sign for the future, Mendoza thought; the boy had the stomach of a sailor. The Northeast Trades pounded *The Cordoba*, pushing her closer and closer to Icacos Point. Captain Pablo called to Mendoza, who went to the stern, and shouting above the howling wind and the chug-chugging of the engine, he said the wind was pushing them too far southwest. The reef south of Soldado Rock would endanger them. He told Mendoza it would be safer to anchor close to the lighthouse at Icacos Point and cross at first light. Mendoza scratched his head and reluctantly agreed. Pablo sailed a more southerly course and two hours later they saw a flame.

At one o'clock in the morning they were a couple hundred yards off the lighthouse. Pablo stopped the engine and Mendoza and Jimenez cast the anchor overboard, paying out the rope as the anchor sank. When it struck the bottom Mendoza paid out a few more fathoms and fastened the rope to the stanchion on *The Cordoba*'s bow. Mendoza took first watch allowing Pablo and Jimenez to sleep; he sat on the bow watching the huge waves go by and observed the spray when they crashed against the Icacos shoreline.

The rising and falling of *The Cordoba* over the huge waves loosened the anchor on the seabed and slowly she headed towards the shore. Mendoza, whose mind had drifted off to his contract in Venezuela, did not notice the drag.

Norman Coutou was the first villager to see *The Cordoba*. Norman was a learned, respectable man of African descent who lived in quarters close to the lighthouse. He worked with the colonial government and doubled as mailman by day and lighthouse keeper by night. Coutou collected mail from the steamer that came to Icacos once a week and delivered it on horseback to villagers and estates in the Icacos and Fullerton districts. In those days the lighthouse was a simple structure. It consisted of a long pole cast into a square concrete platform. The pole was held in place by four cable guide-lines, shackled to four, stout concrete pillars on its outskirts. On the pole were pegs for climbing. At the top of the pole was a huge basket, cradling a tin bowl, covered by a glass shade.

Norman made three trips up the pole: at six o'clock, ten o'clock and at two in the morning. On the six o'clock climb Norman took a five-gallon container filled with kerosene, a potato sack and a long piece of rope. His wife, Emelda, accompanied him on this routine. Norman would wrap the potato sack around his waist, weave the length of rope around it and scale the pole. Once inside the basket he slackened the rope and lowered the end to his wife. Emelda tied the rope to the handle of the kerosene container and Norman hoisted it into the basket. He lifted the huge glass shade and removed the wick from the night before. Carefully, he rolled the potato sack into a wick then placed it into a slot above the bowl, with three quarters of the wick in the bowl and the other quarter in the air. Norman then opened the container and filled the tin bowl with kerosene. He took his box of matches out of his pocket and lit the top of the wick and when the flame burned constant he replaced the glass shade. He remained a few minutes scrutinizing the flame then he stood in the basket and surveyed the sea. Satisfied, he descended under Emelda's watchful eyes. On the ten and two o'clock climb, Norman returned with a potato sack to change the wick since it burned itself out every four hours, but the five gallons of kerosene lasted the night.

It was on one of these two o'clock climbs that Norman noticed the little boat. The wind was fierce and Norman strained as he inched up the pole. Inside the basket, he removed the glass shade. Immediately, the wind extinguished the flame. He rolled up the potato sack and replaced the wick. He took the matches from his pocket, angled his back against the wind, took four matchsticks from the box, scratched them on the sulfur and lit the wick in one try. Norman replaced the shade and smiled at his competence. He watched the flame as it flickered. When it steadied itself he straightened and, as was customary, stood in the basket surveying the rough sea. At first he saw just the shimmering light of *The Cordoba's* lantern as it bobbed in the billowing swells. As his eyes acclimatised, he discerned the silhouetted shape of the craft.

The boat's proximity to the shore worried Norman. Maybe the anchor was adrift. Surely the huge waves would toss her to the shore and destroy her in minutes. Norman leaned over the side of the basket, cupped his palms to his mouth and hollered. No response. Norman hollered again. Emelda came running from the quarters, her ankle-length nightgown blowing wildly, revealing her thighs.

'Quick!' Norman shouted above the bashing waves, as he raced down the pole in the gusty winds. 'Go back to the quarters and fetch kerosene and a sack!'

Emelda returned with the items. Norman took the articles from her and raced down to the shore. He stopped at the water's edge, dropped the sack on the sand and drenched it with kerosene. Grabbing a handful of matchsticks, he angled his back against the wind and scratched them furiously. The sulphur burst into flame but was no match against the wind. Norman crouched on his knees, trying to block out the wind; another try. Norman held the flame to the sack which burst into flames, singeing his eyebrows. In the howling wind, Norman held one end of the flaming sack and began waving it, until it burned his hand. He peered at the little craft.

The Northeast Trades blew animated voices across the water towards Norman. He heard the reluctant grumble of the engine as someone started it and the silhouettes of two men raced to the bow and began pulling in the anchor. Norman laughed and raced up the beach for he knew that he had saved the little craft from certain destruction. He put his hands on Emelda's shoulders and danced around her, both overjoyed as they watched the little craft heading further out to safe anchorage. They sat on a sand bank between the coconut trees and the beach, the wind howling and blowing sand into their eyes. Norman rubbed his eyes with the back of his wrist then looked up at the sky with its hint of a lovely moon and twinkling stars; perfect tranquillity up there, he thought, while the tempest raged below.

The sun rose lazily in a pink haze over the rocks in Columbus Bay. *The Cordoba* sat quietly as the calm waters lapped lazily at her sides. Mendoza marvelled at the change: from a raging tempest during the night to a perfect calm at sunrise. He had brewed his coffee and was sipping it. He glanced at his son who stood gazing at the estate buildings and tall coconut palms lining the shore. Captain Pablo was checking the engine, an old rag in one hand and a dipstick in the next. He wiped the dipstick clean, inserted it into its slot and removed it again. The oil level was good. He took up a bar, placed it on the nut at the front of the engine and began the cranking process, but the engine refused to start. He tried again, but nothing.

Mendoza cursed and flicked the dregs from his cup into the water. He took the cranking bar from Pablo and vainly tried his luck. When Mendoza cursed under his breath and spat into the sea, Pablo backed off to the gunwale, slipped the empty rum bottle into the water then he circled the engine looking for defects. Halfway around he discovered a broken part and showed it to Mendoza who retrieved an old leather-bound kit with spanners and tested each on the nuts around the broken part until he had the right one. He slackened and examined the part. It was broken beyond repair. Mendoza looked from the broken part to the estate buildings. Perhaps he could source a replacement. He would lower the skiff and go ashore with Jimenez.

Mendoza took the key and opened the strongbox. He removed a fistful of gold coins and placed them in his pocket. They lowered the skiff into the water then Jimenez held on to the side of *The Cordoba* and lowered himself into the skiff. Mendoza bent over and passed the broken part to him. He took one of the gold coins from his pocket and tossed it to Pablo then he got into the skiff. Father and son paddled towards the shore, as Pablo sat on the bow of *The Cordoba* and waved, wishing he could go with them: he was out of rum. As his thirst grew he imagined a rumshop somewhere between those coconut trees.

When the skiff landed, Mendoza and Jimenez removed their shoes, rolled up their trousers and got out. Mendoza pulled the rope tied to the bow and, with Jimenez grunting at the stern, they angled the skiff between the trees. They put on their shoes, rolled down their trousers and walked towards the buildings.

Mr. Ponton Chevalier, manager of the Constance Coconut Estate, was on his morning rounds when he encountered Mendoza and Jimenez. He greeted them cheerfully. Mendoza, by means of sign and the English he knew, explained his dilemma, showing Chevalier the broken part. Mr. Chevalier, a kind man of French descent, donned his spectacles. He looked at the part and knew he didn't have it, since it was from a Peta engine and Constance used Delcos. But the St Marie Estate in Bonasse Village used Peta engines and Mr. Bobby Grey, the manager there, was his good friend. Chevalier wrote a note and gave it to Mendoza, loaned him two horses and sent along his fifteen-year-old son, Mitchell Chevalier, on his horse to guide them to the estate in Cedros.

That morning, at quarter past ten, the fishing foursome was removing the branches concealing the *Tetanic*. The mission was twofold: eager to catch more fish, they also wanted a closer look at the strange craft anchored off the coast. Moving with urgency they launched the *Tetanic*. They dug in their paddles, found their rhythm and navigated towards the vessel. They intended to get close, circle, scrutinise and return to the spot where they fished the day before.

They stopped within shouting distance of the craft. A small man on the bow waved to them. Encouraged, the men paddled towards him. Once alongside, Manbode and Rambir held on to the gunwale of *The Cordoba* steadying the *Tetanic* alongside. Pablo smiled and opened his hands in greeting. He fisted his right hand, inclined his head backwards and repeatedly jerked his thumb towards his open mouth. Manbode understood immediately: the man wanted rum. He released his grip on *The Cordoba*'s gunwale, turned to the Venezuelan and, with both hands, shaped a rum bottle.

Captain Pablo's eyelids fluttered. He smiled and shook his head: '¡Sí, sí!'

He reached into his pocket, took out the gold coin and passed it to Manbode whose eyes gleamed as he looked at the gold piece in his palm. Quickly, he pocketed it.

'You want-am rum?' Manbode nodded. 'We go bring-am rum fo yu.'

They paddled towards the shore, Chaitram, Rambir and Padam straining their muscles to quickly complete this errand so they could go fishing. Manbode left the raft and, heading towards the estate, looked at the coin, swearing he must have it. At home he had money stashed in an old can, enough to buy two bottles of rum. He'd use that money. Manbode headed to his house then hustled over to Baban's.

'Baban, me want-am two battles Forres' Pa'k,' he said, emptying the contents of the can on the counter.

Baban opened a cardboard box, lifted out two bottles of rum and eyed Manbode suspiciously. 'Wat! Like yu have-am a salibration, why for yu buy-am so much rum?'

'All time yu mind-am other people bisness,' protested Manbode.

Baban *steupsed*, placed both bottles on the counter and checked the money. He passed the bottles and change to Manbode.

When Pablo saw the rum bottles he licked his lips, smiled and motioned Manbode onboard *The Cordoba*. Once onboard, Manbode realised the man was alone, and he scanned the vessel and discovered the strongbox with its enormous brass padlock. The three men on the raft wanted to go fishing. 'Aye, aye, Manbode, come leh we go,' they chorused. Manbode poked his head over the side. He spotted two row boats from the upper village, fishing a distance from *The Cordoba*.

'Why yu no drop-am anker close by and start-am to fish?' he said. 'Me want-am to speak-am with Panyol mans.'

Meanwhile, Mendoza, Jimenez and Mitchell Chevalier had arrived at the St Marie Estate where Bobby Grey and an Indian man were bent over, measuring cedar logs with a long tape.

'Good day, Mr. Grey,' said Mitchell Chevalier.

Grey looked up. 'Good day, little Chevalier, and also to your friends.' He shook hands with Mitchell who introduced him to the strangers.

Mendoza gave him the letter. Grey adjusted his spectacles, unfolded the letter, read it and asked for the broken part. Mendoza untied the item from his saddle. Grey scratched his head thoughtfully then shouted; a tall, wiry African covered with sweat exited the workshop. He scrutinised the part, nodded and led the visitors to the back of the shop where there was a scrapped Peta engine. The African examined the component and found it serviceable. He disappeared and returned shortly with spanners. Mendoza wanted to pay for the part, but Grey refused, saying, 'Any friend of Chevalier is a friend of mine, but I must insist you three stay for lunch.'

Onboard *The Cordoba*, Captain Pablo concealed one bottle and attacked the other with a flourish, occasionally passing it to Manbode who pretended to drink. The strongbox still transfixed Manbode for he reasoned that a box under lock and key meant precious cargo. He envisioned gold coins, like the one snug in his pocket, and a plan formed in his mind. He scanned *The Cordoba* for other items of interest and his eyes fell on the shotgun. Murder crossed his mind. He thought of shooting the man and making off with the strongbox. Manbode smiled, but discarded the devious thought. He'd have to think of something more subtle.

The rum he bought was forty over proof. Manbode thought one bottle would render the Venezuelan helpless, but he had to get him to drink quickly. Manbode, still pretending, engaged the stranger in a sort of drinking competition. The jolly Venezuelan laughed and sang in his foreign tongue. Manbode gauged Pablo. His behaviour was no different to an estate drunk: they all got happy and spoke too much. As he continued to ply him with liquor, Manbode reasoned that he would soon have the stranger exactly where he wanted him.

The three men on the raft glanced curiously at *The Cordoba*. Manbode moved stealthily about the vessel while the stranger chattered incoherently. Rambir knew Manbode was up to something.

Manbode looked at the Venezuelan with the bottle almost glued to his lips. A fresh breeze had sprung up out of the east. The Venezuelan removed the bottle from his lips and yawned. A long streak of dribble extended and he smiled, his head nodded forward and the saliva deposited itself on the deck and a smaller streak seesawed at the corner of his mouth. He slumped then fell heavily.

Manbode glanced around: the two row boats had slipped out of sight. It was time to act. He threw the shotgun into the sea then shouted to the men on the raft: 'Aye, aye!'

Rambir, sensing Manbode's urgency, quickly pulled in the anchor and they rowed over to *The Cordoba*. Manbode beckoned Rambir to join him. They lowered the strongbox to Padam and Chaitram, who thought it some odd gift, but its heaviness and the stranger's absence bothered him. The *Tetanic* leaned precariously but they shifted the box to the middle and the raft steadied itself. When Manbode drew his cutlass and ordered the *Tetanic* be paddled towards the mangrove swamp east of the estate, Chaitram knew that *that* box wasn't a gift.

At the mangrove Manbode took control. He and Rambir, with Padam following closely behind, hauled the strongbox up the beach. Chaitram, who wanted no part of the box, remained on the raft. The trio returned to Chaitram and together they concealed the *Tetanic*. Manbode loosened the prongs from the anchor and with the stainless steel shaft in his hand they went to the strongbox. Curious, Chaitram followed. Manbode battered the brass lock until it broke. Manbode knelt and flipped the lid. In the shimmering heat, gold coins winked at them. Manbode, Padam and Rambir hunched ravenously over their gleaming treasure, fingers scooping the pile and scattering coins like raindrops. Chaitram, standing aside, saw their greed.

'Manbode, Padam, Rambir,' he pleaded, 'let we take-am gold and carry-am back to Panyol man on boat.'

Manbode drew his cutlass and scrambled Chaitram by his neck. 'You want-am me to cut-am yu throat!'

Padam and Rambir restrained Manbode then the trio stepped aside and whispered among themselves. Chaitram reasoned that although Padam and Rambir had intervened, they would side with Manbode, because they were struck with gold fever. Manbode never released his cutlass. Chaitram regretted building the raft and, stepping back, considered running but, as if reading his thoughts, the men began to circle him. Slowly, they closed in. Chaitram thought of his three sons and dropped to his knees.

'Oh gawd,' he begged, 'please nah kill-am me.'

The trio conferred again and decided they would spare his life on one condition: Chaitram must accept a share of the gold. That way, they thought, he would become an accomplice to the crime and be less inclined to squeal. Chaitram agreed. Manbode seized almost half of the gold for himself then he divided the remainder in three and gave Chaitram an ultimatum:

'Take-am yu share, or me chop-am yu arse to pieces.'

After a sumptuous lunch at the St. Marie Estate, Mendoza thanked Bobby Grey for his kindness. With the serviceable part attached to his saddle, they began the return journey to Constance Estate. A lighthearted Mendoza noticed things he hadn't observed before and pointed out beautiful birds and plants to his son. Mitchell Chevalier rode silently in front.

They passed through the densely wooded area at the back of Fullerton Village, coming over the gently sloping hills, then entered the flat plains with the coconut trees that led to Constance. They reached the huge mangrove swamp, east of the estate. Here the trail to Constance ran along the outskirts of the swamp for almost a mile. A huge alligator, sunning itself, dashed frantically for the water, startling the horses. It took a while for the riders to calm them. Mendoza was clueless that two hundred yards further into the swamp, at that very moment, Manbode, Padam and Rambir were eagerly sharing his gold, while Chaitram accepted his share under duress. They got to the estate around half past three in the afternoon. Mendoza offered to pay for the horses and services Ponton Chevalier had provided but Ponton, like Bobby Grey, declined.

Mitchell Chevalier walked Mendoza and Jimenez to the skiff. Patting him on the back, Mendoza thrust two gold coins into his hand. Mitchell scrutinised the coins, thanked Mendoza and pocketed them. Jimenez shook hands with Mitchell, then he and his father removed their shoes, rolled up their pants and with Mitchell's help they launched the skiff, boarded it and waved goodbye. Mitchell watched them row away and when Mendoza hailed, 'Hola, Juan Pablo,' he turned and walked to the estate.

Captain Pablo wobbled groggily to his feet and grinned vacantly when Mendoza and Jimenez came alongside *The Cordoba.* Mendoza's temper flared immediately: he knew that stupid grin meant intoxication. He tied the skiff and jumped aboard. His eyes raked for the strongbox and his countenance changed. Mendoza glared at Pablo and demanded:

'¿Donde está mi oro?'

Babbling, Pablo gestured in a reassuring way. He looked at the empty spot, then at Mendoza. Confusion replaced the stupid grin. Mendoza rummaged through the boat. The gold was gone. With murder on his mind, he searched for his shotgun. Mendoza swore.

In a fit of anger Mendoza grabbed Pablo and choked him. Pablo offered little resistance as Mendoza exerted pressure. Jimenez grappled with his father but rage powered him. Suddenly, Pablo's body went limp. Mendoza released his hold and Pablo slumped to the deck. Feverishly, Jimenez tried to revive him. He pressed his ear against Pablo's chest, seeking a heartbeat, then he checked his wrist for a pulse. Pablo was dead. Jimenez stared at his father who was foaming and strutting like a bulldog just out of a scuffle.

Mendoza paced the deck, glancing from his son to the body. He tried to think clearly: he had acted too hastily. Pablo was probably the only one who could identify the thieves and now he lay dead. Mendoza took a heavy iron flange from a box and tied it to the dead man's feet. He surveyed the surroundings and Jimenez stood wide-eyed as his father lifted Pablo and slipped him feet first into the water. The boy trembled as the curly hair disappeared under the water leaving air bubbles in its wake. Mendoza returned to his pacing, while Jimenez sobbed softly.

Mendoza stopped, examined the engine, then bent over the side of *The Cordoba* and looked at the part resting in the skiff; he lowered himself and retrieved it. He called to the boy in a trembling voice, passed it to him and climbed into *The Cordoba*. He took up the old leather bag with the spanners and with Jimenez's help they tackled the problem. Mendoza fumbled while tears rolled down his assistant's cheeks but, finally, they inserted the part. He passed the cranking bar to Jimenez who inserted it on the nut and began the cranking process. The engine belched black smoke and roared to life. Mendoza played with the throttle, racing the engine, then pulled the stop wire, silencing the engine. Mendoza and Jimenez boarded the skiff, rowed ashore and located Mr. Ponton Chevalier.

Mendoza laboriously explained to Chevalier about the missing gold, showing him the pieces he had remaining. Chevalier quizzed Mendoza: was anyone else onboard *The Cordoba* when the gold vanished? Mendoza stuttered then denied outright. Chevalier frowned but assured Mendoza he would investigate the missing gold. Mendoza promised to return at first light then he and Jimenez returned to *The Cordoba*. Mitchell, who had overheard the conversation, turned to his father.

'Papa, I am sure there was a next man on *The Cordoba*.'

'Why, Mitch?'

'Because, on approaching the boat, Mr. Mendoza called out to someone named Juan Pablo.'

Seven o' clock that night Chevalier and Mitchell began their investigation. There were five lanes with barracks on the estate settlement. The duo started on the first lane from the seashore going inland. Manbode lived on this row. Chevalier knew about the fishing raft and that Manbode was part of the crew, so when he got to Manbode's house he interrogated him.

'Did you all go with the raft to the Venezuelan boat anchored out to sea?' Mr. Chevalier asked.

'Yes, Bass, we went-am by boat,' Manbode said.

'Was there anyone on board the boat when you got there?'

'Yes, Bass, have-am one mans in boat.'

Mr. Chevalier scratched his head and looked thoughtfully at Mitchell, then back at Manbode. 'Could you describe the man?'

'Yes, Bass, ah small, magar Panyol mans.'

'Did you all go on the boat?'

'No, Bass, the mans give-am me monies to buy-am rum, we go-am back by Baban and buy-am two battles Forres' Pa'k and carry-am back for mans.'

'What type of money did the man give you?'

'We self same paper monies, Bass.'

'With the queen's head?'

'Yes, Bass.'

'Were there other boats in the area?'

'Yes, Bass, have-am row boats from other village.'

When Mr. Chevalier left, Manbode slipped over to Rambir's house on the other lane and instructed him how to answer the boss's questions. Next he went to Padam's. At Chaitram's the atmosphere was ugly. Manbode summoned him outside, warned him and swore if he deviated from the plan, he'd chop off his three sons' heads. Manbode climbed the three steps into the little gallery where Chaitram's three sons stood with their hands on the bannister and, one by one, he ruffled their hair, while his right hand toyed with the cutlass hanging from his waist.

It was almost nine-thirty when Mr. Chevalier ended his investigations. Walking from the fifth lane back to the seashore, he puzzled over his information: the rafts men were the natural suspects but Manbode, Rambir, Padam and Chaitram had corresponding stories. They all mentioned a third person onboard *The Cordoba*, and Chevalier trusted Chaitram; and Baban, the shopkeeper, had verified that Manbode paid for two bottles of rum in local currency. Their stories seemed credible. Why then was Mendoza denying Pablo's existence? The Frenchman concluded that the Venezuelan was hiding something. Working on a sudden hunch, Chevalier and Mitchell trekked towards the lighthouse keeper's quarters on the beach. A lantern lit the house where Norman Coutou was preparing for his ten o'clock climb. Mr. Chevalier called out and Norman and his wife, Emelda, exited. Norman told Chevalier he was out delivering mail all day; Emelda said she had seen the raft and some row boats in *The Cordoba's* vicinity. Mr. Chevalier looked out across the sea: he saw the tiny light of *The Cordoba* as it bobbed in the water. Eeriness pervaded the air. Mr. Chevalier thanked the couple and left. He visited the estate's overseer's house and told him to keep the entire work force in the yard the next morning. As they left the overseer's house, Chevalier peered at a starless sky and felt droplets on his face. He raced his son to their bungalow.

It drizzled for ten minutes then increased to a tropical downpour. Chaitram lay on his bed of rags with his wife Dularie at his side, as the rain beat out its melody against the naked galvanised roof, a melody that would normally draw Chaitram into a bout of lovemaking with *his Dularie*. But tonight the melody sounded like death drums. Dularie raised her head and looked at the three boys lying on the old coconut fibre mattress in the corner. They were asleep. She waited for Chaitram to make his move, but he tossed and turned restlessly.

'Man, eh man,' she whispered, 'you nah want-am ting tonight?'

'Me feel-am tired, gyal,' Chaitram sighed, his mind wrestling with Manbode's threats.

The rain continued its music on the roof. Dularie draped her arm around Chaitram's shoulder and drifted to sleep. Chaitram lay there, wide awake, his instincts telling him the day's events would bring some disaster. He had buried his share of the gold in an earthen jar next to the big hog plum tree close to the pond east of the estate settlement. He wanted to go out in the blinding rain, dig up the jar and take it to the manager, explaining to him exactly what

49

had happened but feared that if he did, Manbode would kill his three sons.

Chaitram tried to control his thoughts but his mind raced in all directions. Carefully, so as not to awaken Dularie, he released himself from her arm and crept to the boys on the old mattress. He looked at them and passed his palm gently over their faces. Then he crawled back to his bed.

He had to save his family. He would lie low and at the earliest opportunity go to the Andalusian Estate, close to Fullerton, where they had housing. He'd ask for work and if accepted move his family there. He knew the conditions were worse than at Constance, but would chance it. He looked at Dularie in her sleep of poverty. He desperately wanted to do better for her and the boys, but, by his own endeavours. Not with stolen gold. He had a funny feeling about the gold and vowed he would never touch it in his lifetime, not even if starvation threatened his family. He hadn't mentioned it, not even to Dularie, and he wasn't going to tell anyone – not now anyway.

The Cordoba was wet. The wind pushed rain into every sleeping corner. Not that it mattered, because the day's events had already sentenced its *two* occupants to a sleepless night. Several times Mendoza got up and worked the hand pump, at times more out of anxiety than need. Pablo's curly hair disappearing under the water haunted Jimenez and he sobbed softly along with the raindrops.

At five thirty in the morning Mendoza and Jimenez boarded the skiff and rowed ashore. Ponton Chevalier was waiting. He had all the estate workers lined up in two rows in front of the estate's workshop. The sun began to peep through the thick foliage of coconut branches. Chevalier took Mendoza aside.

'Did you or did you not have a third man onboard?'

Suddenly, Mendoza did not comprehend English.

They returned to the estate workers and Chevalier addressed them: 'These gentlemen are missing a box of gold from their boat. If anyone knows about the gold please step forward.'

A tense silence followed but no one moved. Manbode, Rambir and Padam stared at Chaitram and when their eyes met, Manbode made a cutthroat sign. Chevalier repeated the question. More silence.

Mendoza turned to Chevalier and said, 'Señor, eef dey doan give me back my gole, something terr'ble goin to come apon dees estate in twenti wan days.'

'Señor Mendoza, are you threatening us?' Chevalier scowled. 'What about Pablo? Where's Pablo?'

Mendoza cursed Chevalier in Spanish. He called to Jimenez and they stormed towards the skiff. On *The Cordoba* Mendoza faced facts: it was no use, the estate workers would never talk and if Chevalier, that inquisitive French bastard, went to the authorities, he could face a murder charge. Suppose the body washed ashore? Mendoza was scared. He had to leave for Venezuela immediately and knew whom he was going to see once there.

The Cordoba departed Icacos, heading for the mainland. Mendoza skirted Soldado Rock and its large reef then put *The Cordoba* on a beeline for the Pedernales River mouth. He bypassed the villages and headed straight for La Bruha's clearing. She was on the river bank, crouched over her walking stick. She seemed to be waiting for Mendoza. On her head she balanced a silver plate and on it was a twinkling light.

The day after *The Cordoba* departed, Chaitram Singh left immediately after his morning task for the Andalusian Estate, four miles northeast of the Constance Estate. He was afraid for his family. He had seen how Manbode, Rambir and even his cousin, Padam, looked at him menacingly when Chevalier and Mendoza were investigating the missing gold. He could not remain among them. He had to move out.

Chaitram skirted the seashore to get to the Andalusian Estate. Trudging along he glanced behind every so often. At the cemetery off Constance, which was now almost on the beach, he observed the exposed edge of a coffin. Although he knew huge waves caused the erosion Chaitram interpreted it as a bad omen. He quickened his pace until he reached the area where the *Tetanic* was hidden. He saw little fingers of smoke rising into the air. He hastened to the spot.

His raft was burnt to ashes. He knelt on the hot sand, tears streaming, hands unconsciously sifting through the hot ruins and clutching charred bits of binding wire. Chaitram's spirit was broken. The raft was the one bright spot in his life. He had built it with love for his family. Months of planning had gone into it. His only desire was a better family life. He rose, tears gushing, but steeled with determination he raced towards the Andalusian Estate where the manager promised him a job.

Next day, Chaitram hired old man Soomai and his bull cart, loaded his family together with dented pots, pans, a cage with common fowls, broken possessions and rags, and quietly left Constance. A confused and teary eyed Dularie went along blindly. Chaitram looked back at estate workers gathered close by, whispering among themselves. Sadly, he waved. Born at Constance, it was the only home he knew. These were *his* people. Part of him was dying, but instinct told him flight was the key to survival.

Chaitram's departure was welcome news to Manbode, Rambir and Padam. Now, they felt secure to go to their personal cache and lift a few coins. The trio hatched a plan to go to a far-off place to spend it where no one could detect them. Ponton Chevalier was suspicious about the sudden departure of *The Cordoba*, the flight of Chaitram and now the voyage of Manbode, Rambir and Padam to San Fernando by steamer. He thought restlessly about dispatching a letter with Norman Coutou to the authorities in Port of Spain so they could investigate the matter but, considering the scenario, decided to let the mystery evolve.

Moon, the crab catcher, saw it first. At ten o'clock, returning along the beach from the mangrove swamp east of Constance, he noticed the light coming, from Venezuela. Moon thought it was a pitching star but the light travelled steadily, low over the black water. Moon was puzzled as the light drew closer. Bigger than a star, he thought, and twinkling just like one. It approached the lighthouse. Terrified, Moon threw the bag of crabs off his head and darted home.

Coutou, inside the lighthouse's basket, saw the light next when it zoomed overhead. He marvelled and thought that if he captured such a light and placed it in the lighthouse's shade he'd never have to climb again. He leaned against the basket and looked as the light headed to the barracks. It circled the houses, as if surveying them, then turned towards him. Norman was in awe and as it zoomed over, a cold tremor swept through his body.

Next morning news of the light spread quickly, for others had seen it. Chevalier, familiar with stories of superstitious sightings, chuckled at the gossip, but later that day when he heard it from the lighthouse keeper he became curious, for he knew Norman was reliable. At home he consulted his almanac: twenty one days had elapsed since *The Cordoba* sailed. Chevalier wondered if *that* light had anything to do with Mendoza's threats.

Next night the light returned. At midnight the estate watchman saw it approaching The Serpent's Mouth. It slowed then headed for Manbode's house, circling it menacingly. Then it stood still – about twenty feet over the barrack. Suddenly, as if descending a ladder, down, down it came, bumped once against the roof then shot off like a rocket towards Venezuela.

In the morning, Manbode's wife tried to rouse him but he was dead. Later, they found the night watchman wandering the seashore aimlessly, unable to speak.

Two days later the light was back. Ponto Chevalier awakened to the barking of the estate dogs at three in the morning. He shifted his curtain: the light was descending on Rambir's roof. Ponton's hair stood on end. The light bounced onto the roof, rose into the air and began to circle Padam's house then started its descent. Chevalier shivered to his knees and began to pray. At three-thirty a scream erupted at Rambir's; two minutes later, wailing engulfed Padam's house. Chevalier, still in prayer, was afraid to go out. At four o'clock, when the estate came alive, he ventured out. Rambir and Padam were dead.

Next night, during the wake for the departed, an old woman shrieked. Mourners looked up and saw the light rocketing towards the estate. People scattered in all directions. Slowly, the light circled the settlement then bolted towards Venezuela never to be seen again.

Chaitram and his three sons sat on the steps of his Andalusian barrack. Behind him, Dularie in her ragged dress heated dhal and rice on the fireside. Common fowls clucked around the yard. He had just come in from a hard *day's* work. Things were tougher here than at Constance. He knew about the deaths of Padam, Manbode and Rambir one month ago. He mumbled a silent prayer, thanking God for sparing his life. He reached over, wiped snot from his sons' noses and flicked golden mucus to a black cock with a red comb.

Bend Foot Bailey

It had this fellar named Libert Bailey who they use to call "Bend Foot Bailey" because, from his knees down, his feet were bent so bad that his toes on one foot always faced the toes on the other foot. Now Bailey really born in La Romaine to a girl called Wanita Bailey, a country girl from Icacos that get a work to mind some little children for a "modern" working couple.

Next door to the people had a saga boy named Taffy and he didn't waste no time. Right away he promised Wanita the moon and the stars. In a couple months, Wanita belly start to rise like if she drinking yeast, and right away Taffy's moon start to dim and he stars begin to disappear, because Taffy in the swelling belly business; he not family oriented. By the time Libert born Taffy cut out and run, taking he moon and stars with him and leaving poor Wanita behind in total darkness. The couple that Wanita worked for felt sorry. They allowed her to keep her job and the baby.

Very early Wanita noticed the problem with Libert's feet. The "doctor" told her that Libert would need an expensive operation to correct them, but the possibility existed that by wearing a certain type of boots they might correct themselves over a period of time. Being a poor single parent Wanita went with the possibility. She bought a pair of boots but soon realised that instead of the boots straightening Libert's feet, Libert's feet were bending the boots. She bought another pair with the same results. And then she decided that "what has to be must be." And that is how Libert's feet remained bent like two crook sticks. They never straightened.

When Libert was five years old Wanita get an opportunity to go to The U.S.A. and work. She couldn't take Libert, so she turn to the one, living relative that she had, her father, Old Man Rocky, who lived in Icacos. Wanita drop the child off by Rocky, catch a plane and buss it off to New York.

Old Man Rocky led a lonely life in a little wooden hut about two hundred feet from the pitch road, tending a few animals and planting some crops for his living. The hut stood in a clearing which was littered with a couple of fruit trees. Old Man Rocky had a talent. He was a first class guitar player, but he played only to the few school children who came to pick fruits from his trees, or, sometimes to ease his own melancholy. To Old Man Rocky, his grandson was a more than welcome arrival.

Libert was of age for school and soon after his arrival Old Man Rocky hustled off and enrolled him at the Icacos primary school. Libert's early school days was more of an education in warfare than books. From day one they called him Bend Foot Bailey and teased him, and he fought them. They always beat him, because he was only one and they were many. With all having bigger brothers and sisters in higher classes, they fought in clans, so he went home to Old Man Rocky on that first day, and many days that followed, crying and battered. That was why Old Man Rocky decided to teach Libert to play the guitar, to help him ease his little mind.

Every Christmas Wanita would full up a barrel with clothes and other goodies and ship it to her father and son. When Bend Foot Bailey was ten, a guitar arrived in a barrel. Old Man Rocky was elated because with two guitars it was now much easier to teach his grandson. In no time at all Bend Foot Bailey start to make that guitar talk and say some things that nobody ever thought a guitar could say. When Old Man Rocky and Bend Foot Bailey start to caress them strings and sing on a Friday evening, people passing on the pitch road would hear the music and follow it into the clearing and sit there spellbound, listening to the sweet sounds that the old man and his little grandson were coaxing out of them strings. It wasn't long before people buying their rum on Friday afternoons and hustling off to Rocky's house, sitting in the clearing to hear music. Some fellars so boldface that they taking along their girlfriends and dancing late into the night because the music was free.

But guitar playing was only a pastime for Bend Foot Bailey. His real ambition was to be a footballer. And Bailey didn't allow those bent feet to keep him back at all. When Bailey walking the road he kicking anything in sight: coconut shell, cigarette boxes, pieces of paper; even small stones feel the wrath of Bailey's ambition. If Bailey meet a tin can in the road, he consider that a Christmas present, and he kicking it for over a mile before he get fed up. But is when rain fall in the night that Bailey used to get his real kicks. He use to borrow his grandfather's flashlight, and he out on the pitch road, flashing and kicking crapaud (frogs) left, right and centre.

From the time Bailey was nine he trying out for the school's football team and when Bailey reach fifteen and sit his school leaving exam, he still couldn't make the reserve bench. Bailey come big man, he try out with every football side in the Cedros-Icacos district but he still can't make a team. He wasn't a bad player; he use to confuse a lot of defenders with his bend foot and awkward style, but people just didn't want any bend foot fellar playing football on their team.

Well, is now self Bailey start kicking things. He and Old Man Rocky start falling out, because he kicking Rocky's shoes all over the house and he using the gallery door as a goal post—so he would dribble round a couple chairs, line up the goal post and bam! Rocky's shoes through the door, over the gallery banister and out into the yard, and Bailey bawling "G-o-a-l!" Wednesday morning Rocky getting ready to go and collect his old age pension, can't find his shoes anywhere, cursing Bailey in patois, and is only then Bailey remember the shoes outside and running to retrieve it—Rocky shoes full with water because rain fall during the night, so is more cuss. But Bailey never back-answered his grandfather.

In those days, Icacos had some wicked little boys, but none as disrespectful as Patrick and Bolan; these two does back-answer grandfather, father and mother too. And the funny thing is the two of them always liming together. The old people in the village swear that these two boys have no respect for God or man. One day Patrick and Bolan see the Bailey coming down a lonely road, and right away Bolan decide to pull a fast one on the Bailey.

'You want to see something?' Bolan grinned and, before Patrick could answer, he took down his pants and do the second number in the middle of the road. Quickly, he took a coconut shell and covered it over so that nothing could be seen, and the two of them hid behind some bushes.

This time Bailey coming up the road in a jovial mood, his two bend foot zigzagging and he strumming his guitar and singing a jumpy number: 'If I had a hammer, I would of hammer in the morning.' And he bounce up the coconut shell smack in the middle of the road. This time Patrick and Bolan hiding in the bush and watching the Bailey with great expectations. The Bailey couldn't believe his good luck. He looked at the coconut shell; the guitar string go 'pling!' And a smile spread over his face.

He stopped.

He reversed back.

He rest down the guitar.

Biting his lips he rubbed his palms together.

He take aim.

And he take off! his two feet flip-flopping as he went, and with a kick that would of scored a goal in any world cup fixture, he connected with the coconut shell. The next thing you know Bolan's numbers all over the Bailey's shirt and pants, and he start cussing in patois. Patrick and Bolan had to hold down each other's mouth behind the bushes lest the Bailey should hear their laughter.

But not even this incident could blunt the Bailey's ambition.

The Bailey's walk could easily be compared to that of a crab–if you see him walking for the first time you bound to laugh. One time the Bailey won a dance competition and he wasn't even taking part. It use to have this big St. Peter's Day celebration in

Icacos. People used to come from all over to join in the fun: greasy pole, boat race and jam session like that. This year in question they had a dance competition right on the main road in front of Harris's shop. The dancers doing their thing on the road, and the judges looking for a winner. The Bailey ain't know what was going on. He walking casually in the middle of the road looking for things to kick. He passed right through the competition, dodging dancers, his eyes glued to the ground looking for something to kick. The chief judge got all excited: 'Check out the moves on that guy in the blue shirt and straw hat!' Instantly the panel agreed with her and had the music stopped. The chief judge picked up the microphone: 'Let the fellar in the blue shirt and straw hat step forward to the podium, please.' Bailey, ain't know is he they talking about, kept on walking. "Look! Look! The music has stopped and he's still dancing," shouted the chief judge and she raced after him and brought him back to the podium. The next thing you know the Bailey have a big trophy in his hand and money in his pocket.

Every year it used to have a football match between Icacos and Bonasse. It was the crowning fixture on the Cedros football calendar and it use to be more like a war than a football match. Bonasse have some real good players. Since the inauguration of the match, five years ago, Icacos never won, in fact the best result they ever get was the year before, when they manage to lose by only one goal.

This particular year, a certain factor seemed to be tilting the scales in Icacos' favour. The factor came in the form of a priest. The Icacos church, normally manned by a white Irish priest, saw a changing of the guards. Back to Ireland goes father O'Connor and down comes the first local priest, a St. Mary's educated boy christened Michael Thursday. Thursday was a firebrand, a real livewire and he came with Intercol (Inter College) football fever in his blood. He was one of the better players from St. Mary's in the days when they and St. Benedict's Boys used to do battle. Father Thursday arrived in Icacos two months and a week before this famous match. The next day he hear about it, about how Icacos always getting their tail cut. He say:

'Nah! This is my parish now! Enough is enough!'

And he jump in the fray and take over the coaching of the Icacos team. Sunday morning, during mass, Father Thursday declared his new portfolio as coach of the Icacos team. He invited tall, short, fat, skinny, the quick and the half-dead (everyone!) to the Icacos Recreation Ground from Monday evening at three o'clock to register and train. A twenty-four-year-old Bailey, sitting there in church, his bend foot kicking the pew in front of him, began smiling from ear-to-ear, seeing this as his chance to finally get onto a football team. That night rain fall; the Bailey ain't sleep—the next morning somebody count ninety one dead crapaud on the pitch road in front Old Man Rocky's clearing.

Monday evening twenty-nine, feverish fellars show up at the Icacos Recreation Ground. Father Thursday line them up in two lines—the Bailey in the front row. Squinting, Father Thursday take one look at the Bailey's feet and then he look at the keen interest on his face, and Father get the feeling that he venturing down break heart alley, but he done take the job and he have plenty faith.

So there it was when Father not on the pulpit pelting fire and brimstone at the congregation, he out on the recreation ground, in shorts and football socks, putting the villagers through rigorous exercises and teaching them sound footballing skills like skate tackles, offside traps and one-touch passes. You won't believe the amount of young ladies that use to find their way to the recreation ground just to get a peep at father, out of his gown and in them short pants; and some of them so shameless, they saying to one another, "You ain't find Father have sexy legs!"

One month after the start, Father sit down in the night with pen and paper to trim his squad to twenty two players. Every now and then he marking down a name, then he rolling the paper into a scroll to kill a mosquito that kept attacking his ankle. When Father reach twenty one, he remember the Bailey and he can't find it in his priestly heart to drop the bend foot fellar because the boy have too much enthusiasm, so he put in his name last on the list. Father lay there that night thinking of ways to improve the Bailey's game. He ran well enough and Father had noticed that he often tied up the opposition with his awkward style–maybe he could work on that. Finally Father realised what had been eluding him: Bailey was trying to play as a person with normal feet. If he used his disability to his advantage, he might create more problems for the opposition with his awkwardness. Father Thursday smiled and dropped off to sleep.

The next day, at the recreation ground, Father took out his list of twenty two players and began to read it out. The Bailey's heart was sinking slowly but when he heard his name, his countenance brightened and he made a sound like a guitar string: "pling!"

Now Father's plan was to divide the twenty two players into two teams of eleven, and play these two teams against each other on training days. In this way he would be able to have a better look at all the players, and then he would select his final fourteen in two week's time. Father pulled Bailey aside after he read the names and said to him:

'Bailey, what I notice is that you are trying to play like… like your feet are normal but… they are not. You should run like a bend-footed person, kick like a bend-footed person and dribble like a bend-footed person. What I am trying to say is, use your disability to your advantage.'

Bailey, grinning from ear-to-ear, said, 'What you mean father, is that you want me to do it my way.'

'Exactly, Bailey! Exactly! Do it the way only Bend Foot Bailey could do it.'

Then Father organised the two teams, placed the whistle to his mouth and started the game. Immediately Bailey made an impact. There he was sending the opposing defenders this way and that, as he bobbed and weaved between them with his awkward style. Father Thursday stood and looked on in awe, his heart pounding in his chest, as the Bailey began exploiting his uniqueness for the first time. In the two weeks that followed the Bailey improved so much that Father Thursday had no choice but to include him in the final fourteen.

With his final team chosen Father Thursday's training sessions intensified. Fellars complained, tempers flared. Father so involved and high-strung that he and a suddenly lazy player called

Toto Crab nearly break a fight. *Toto Crab* say: 'Father, what you need is a nice little priestess to help you simmer down, boy,' and the players doubled over in laughter; even Father laughed at himself.

Father hear Bonasse playing a practice match so he gone to spy out their team. Bonasse have some players that take his breath away. It have a fellar name *Tax* and a next one name *Crevedo*, them two fellars fast like lightning and talk about shots— these two kicking so hard that it frightening! And the goalkeeper, the man is a real dream, he diving at anything—*Lagoon Shark* they call him.

Next day, during training, Father singled out his two fastest defenders, a fellow named Frankie Johlai and a next one named John Findley. He start to put things in place to deal with the threat of *Tax* and *Crevedo*. After practice Father have Johlai and Findley playing catch with each other. First he have Johlai chasing Findley around the field and when he catch him he have Findley chasing Johlai, and both of them wondering what the hell is all the chasing about. But secretly Father preparing them to do a man-to-man marking on *Tax* and *Crevedo*, and every evening the chasing continue. One week before the match and Father pleased with the preparations. Johlai and Findley running like two race horse, the goalkeeper, Leo Nurse, looking good but the big surprise is Bend Foot Bailey.

The Bailey brimming with confidence, wiggling and worming his way between defenders, the only thing is that he a little slow, but Father Thursday have a plan. He going to hold him until the Bonasse team get a little tired.

Sunday morning before the match, Father leading the congregation in prayers for the football team. Hindu, Muslim, Catholics and otherwise, the whole team of fourteen line up there in the front pew to receive the blessings of Father and the congregation because everybody know how things could get rough when it come to this football match.

Now normally, Icacos and Bonasse people does live like first cousins. I mean, an Icacos young boy could go to the Bonasse cinema to watch a movie and after the movie he might walk a little Bonasse chick home, only to find out when he get back to the cinema that the taxi that he come in leave him. He now have to stand up there by the cinema bridge, hoping to see a car passing that might take him to Icacos, but that would hardly happen, because at that hour of the night, nearly everybody sleeping. So the young fellar just marking time on the bridge because he stranded. Suddenly, you will see a curtain shift across the road and a voice will call out into the darkness:

'Where you from, boy?'

'Icacos.'

'Who is you father?'

'*Whiteman.*'

'*Whiteman?* Oh, you mean the fellar that does climb the coconut trees with the set of pretty daughters.'

'Yes, that same one.'

'Well, come on out of the dew, son, you wouldn't get anything to go home at this hour. Come, we have a spare bed here, you could sleep with us.'

And you gone over only to realise is Old Lady Marianne and her husband, Mr. Mano. Before you know it, you in a nice soft bed sleeping. In the morning when you get up Mrs Marianne done have the table set with some nice fry bake, saltfish and cocoa tea. You eat you belly full and when you leaving they telling you, don't forget to tell *Whiteman* and you mother Mrs Melda hello for we.

That is how Bonasse and Icacos people does live. Is a family thing. They never allow one another to be stranded. But when you hear these two villages playing football all that cousin business done. Is war!

Sunday evening, the Cedros Recreation Ground in all its glory, smooth and green like a carpet, the atmosphere electrifying. All of Bonasse and Icacos turn out to support their teams. People from other villages, like Granville, Chatham and Fullerton, come out in their numbers to view the impending battle. Two policemen were on horseback clearing people from the playing area. The old truck bringing the Icacos players arrived at the venue. Some of the Icacos players looking at the pretty girls, but the Bailey looking at the Cedros Recreation Ground from the back of the old truck, like an artist does look at a new canvas when he about to paint a masterpiece.

The players came off the truck and the two teams lined up on the field. The Bonasse team was in blue and white, Icacos in all black. A calypsonian fellow, Conrad Valentine, sang the national anthem while everyone stood at attention. Then Patrick Gopaul, the referee, blew the whistle to begin the war.

From the time the ball touch *Tax* and *Crevedo* were on the attack. The Icacos defence was in disarray. Within three minutes their goalkeeper, Leo Nurse, had to tip a hot one over the bar from *Crevedo*; corner to Bonasse. The Bonasse left-winger curled a dangerous ball across the face of the goal and *Tax* connect with a flying header, but Leo Nurse dived to the far post, plucking the ball out of the air and clutching it to his chest. He cursed his defenders and took a goal kick that sent the ball deep into the Cedros half, but back it came and Bonasse have the Icacos goal under siege. *Tax* and *Crevedo* like they have Apache blood, they raiding with precision and is only the brilliance of Leo Nurse that keeping the wolf from the door. Half-an-hour play gone, the score nil-nil, thanks mainly to the heroics of the Icacos goalkeeper. Gradually, Johlai and Findley, the Icacos defenders, started to get into the game, dismantling the endeavors of *Tax* and *Crevedo*, with an animated Father Thursday shouting instructions from the reserve bench. The Icacos captain, a fellow named Wilfred Nurse, began asserting himself in midfield, and slowly, Icacos began to inch their way into the game.

Bailey on the reserve bench, kicking the ground and watching Father anxiously and wondering when the priest would send him on. Father, sensing his anxiety, reassures him:

'Don't worry, Bailey, I have big plans for you.'

Five minutes to halftime, the score still nil-nil, Bonasse start to up the tempo again but the Icacos defence rise to the occasion. Halftime, the score still nil-nil. Father takes his team to the back of the pavilion and reads the riot act. The teams freshens up and they are back out onto the field.

The whistle blows and the war is on again. *Crevedo* and *Tax* on the war path. They stretching the Icacos defence to its limit, but Leo Nurse still standing strong. After ten minutes Father pulls out his ace. He takes off one of his strikers, a fellow called *Tokes*, and sends on The Bailey.

This is the moment that Bailey had been waiting on for twenty four long years. But all around the ground, people were laughing as Bailey hobbled out to the middle.

"Jesus, all y'u look! Icacos sending on Bend Foot Bailey!" shouted a Bonasse supporter, drawing hilarious laughter from the crowd.

The Bailey dazzled from the word go. He wiggling and worming his way through the Bonasse defence and handing off accurate passes to the other two Icacos strikers. Slowly, the pressure begins to mount on Bonasse.

Suddenly The Bailey picks up a ball in centerfield and starts to dribble towards the Bonasse goal; he dances a man to the left then turns him to the right and leaves the man flat on his buttocks; the crowd roars and an Icacos supporter yells, "All y'u see what Bend Foot Bailey could do!" This time The Bailey advancing towards the goal (the Bonasse defence panicking), going past another defender and is only the last stopper and the goalkeeper, *Lagoon Shark*, in his way. The last stopper, a fellar name *Guava Root*, decide that no bend-foot-fellar that running like a bow-foot-spider going to make a laughing stock out of him, so he gone in with a fierce tackle and send ball and The Bailey flying into the air. Referee blowing whistle like mad and a Bonasse supporter bawling: 'Jeez-an-ages *Guava Root*! You go kill Bend Foot Bailey!' Father Thursday rushed out onto the field and in no time he have The Bailey up and ready to go. A penalty was awarded to Icacos. Silence around the ground. Icacos captain, Wilfred Nurse, steps up to take the kick— *Lagoon Shark* is ready in the Bonasse goal. The referee sounds the whistle, and Wilfred kicks!

Oh no! Straight against the uprights, and the ball ricochets back into play. Bonasse has it now and they are making a run to the

Icacos goal. *Crevedo* passes it to another teammate, Didier, and he shoots! Straight into the arms of Leo Nurse.

Five minutes to go, the Icacos left-winger, Tony Farrel, is making an inspiring run down the left flank; The Bailey reads the play and starts making a run towards the Bonasse goal! The left-winger goes past a defender and is approaching the corner flag; he raises his head and sees The Bailey making his run into the Bonasse penalty area; he crosses the ball; The Bailey flips backward; the goalkeeper, *Lagoon Shark*, sees the flip and thinks, oh, he's going for the bicycle kick, so instantly he dives for the far post, but *Lagoon Shark* made no allowance for that bend foot, and The Bailey's toe just barely hook that ball and send it the other way; *Lagoon Shark* on the ground and he watching the ball bumping s-l-o-w-l-y towards the near post; now he's on his knees creeping quickly towards the ball; the ball seem to be slowing down; he thinks he will get it now and he makes another desperate dive, but the ball just eludes him and rolls gently into the net. "G-o-a-l!"

The Icacos supporters are running wild! Not even the police and their horses could stop them now, they are on the field and lifting The Bailey into the air. The score: Icacos, one: Bonasse, nil.

The remaining minutes see Bonasse go into all out attack but the Icacos defence is holding up like a wall. They are into injury time now, the referee is looking at his watch and suddenly he blows his whistle to end the game. The score: Icacos, one; Bonasse, nil.

That night it was celebration time when the Icacos team got back home. Old and young congregated on the Icacos junction, Old Man Rocky came with the two guitars, and he and The Bailey, backed up by a fellar named *Red Ganze* on a bongo drum, had the players and villagers dancing on the Icacos junction; even Father Thursday start to do a little jig. Miss Ivy come with a ring stove and put up a big pot of *pelau* to cook, right there on the junction. The lime went on until midnight and then people went to their homes. As soon as The Bailey reached home he jumped on his bed and dropped off to sleep.

The Bailey having a dream three o'clock that morning: he in this big hall with hundreds of crapaud. The hall have a podium and King Crapaud sitting up there on his throne.

'Libert Bailey, step forward,' said the king and The Bailey went up on the podium. 'Libert Bailey, you have practised on us for years and today you have perfected yourself and made us proud. We therefore wish to knight you into the Order of The Crapaud. Kneel before me to receive this honour.'

The Bailey kneeled before the King Crapaud and the king took out a big flashlight, just like Rocky's, and smashed it against The Bailey's head.

Bailey flew up and his hand went to his head, but he realised then that he was only dreaming. So he vowed there and then never to kick another crapaud again.

The strong angel

My parents were getting along in age when I came into the world. Married in their late twenties it was when she was thirty-nine and he forty-one that I was born. No one came before, or after, so I was the object of their existence. It was quite easy to understand the joy that I must have brought to them, but my mother explained to me later on that I came with a bit of anxiety also. How apprehensive she was when she found out that she was pregnant and how carefully she examined me for defects after birth. She being a nurse knew that at her age the chances of making a defective child were greater. She thanked God that, more or less, everything was in its right place.

Earliest memories of my parents were ones of overflowing love. Obedience, good manners and virtuous things were taught to me gently, never by harsh words or the use of a whip. I grew into a confident teenager because of their immense love and guidance. At sixteen years of age I would still leave my room in the middle of the night, diving between the two of them and having a cozy sleep until daybreak. Sometimes in the rainy season, when tropical thunderstorms would obliterate midnight's silence and lightning would turn the black of night into day, they would come into my room and cover me with a blanket and each would lie on either side of me and spend the night. Me a big, sixteen-year-old boy, pretending to be asleep, but wide awake, basking in the love of these two beautiful people. We were inseparable, the three of us.

One afternoon I came home from school and found the house deserted. I looked under the mat and found the key. They always left it there if they went out in a hurry. A little while after I heard the car come up the driveway and went outside to meet them. My father stepped out of the car. He looked very tense. He walked around the car and opened the passenger's door for my mother. She was looking rather pale.

"Is something the matter?" I asked.

"Oh, not really," she said.

"Where have you two been?"

"We were out courting, son," she laughed. "We are not too old for that, are we?"

We went inside. My father was unusually quiet. He sat down and began playing with his left ear. He always did this when he had something important to say and was searching for the right words.

"Did you eat your food, son?" asked my mother.

"Not as yet," I replied.

"Tommy, there is something we have to tell you," said my father.

"What is it, dad?"

"Yesterday your mother discovered a lump in her right breast. Today I took her to the doctor and after examining her, he said that we should come back tomorrow for him to remove the lump and send it for testing."

"Oh nothing to worry about, son, probably just a cyst," she said. She brought my food over to where I sat, but somehow my hunger had perished.

The next morning I wanted to go with them.

"It's nothing really, son, simple procedure, local anesthesia, a small gash, out comes the lump, two stitches and back to normal. No reason to miss school and besides you have exams coming up in a couple months," she said.

I went to school, that is my body went but my mind wandered off to the doctor's office and by midmorning I was sent out of the class for not paying attention to the teacher. When I got home that afternoon she showed me the tiny cut with its two neat stitches.

"See what I told you, Tommy? Nothing to worry about."

Two weeks later there was something to worry about. I came home from school and met her sitting there very composed but it was written all over my father's face. I knew it before he said it.

"Your mother has cancer, son."

I was young, but I already knew the dangers of that 'C' word, knew that it was nothing short of a death sentence, and my world fell to pieces.

"Oh, come on, Tommy," she said. "It's not the end of the world and, besides, the doctor says that we have caught it early. He would just have to remove the breast and chances are we would have gotten rid of the whole cancer."

They moved quickly and within a week they made my mother into a one-breasted woman. She knew it was necessary, but I knew that it made her sad. Two weeks after she came out of the hospital I came home early and stumbled on her without her being aware of me; she was looking in the mirror and touching the spot where her right breast would have been. There was immense sadness in her eyes. I would have easily given my two feet if it could have brought back that right breast.

She recovered quickly but went back to the hospital regularly to do numerous tests. After about three months, they pronounced her cancer free. It was great news. That was in January and then came a beautiful year. She went back to work, but on weekends we went everywhere: beaches, cinemas, malls and visiting our family all over the island. Always a charitable person, she got right down to business and my father, Samuel, was a willing accomplice. They would pack food stuff into parcels and she would take them to the health centre where she worked and give them out to the people in need. One day, she came home from work and said, "Samuel, can you imagine a woman came into the health centre today with five children, and every one of them was barefooted?"

"Is that so?" asked my father.

"Yes, it broke my heart," she said.

"Do you know where she lives?" he asked.

"I took an address," she said.

The next afternoon, my father took a piece of string, a penknife, a pen and piece of paper and we went to the village where my mother worked to search for the woman with the barefooted children. It was something I will never forget. They lived in a little mud hut with a thatched roof. She was a single parent. Her man, unable to face up to the hard times they were going through, had cut out and run, leaving her and the children to fend for themselves. Yet they were the most loving children I had ever met. They climbed all over me. My father took out his tools and went to work. Carefully, he measured their feet with the string, cutting it into pieces according to the sizes of their feet, and marked it boy or girl on the paper. The next evening when my father came home from teaching he had five new pairs of shoes in a large white plastic bag. That family became weekly beneficiaries of my parents' generosity.

My exams came along and I did satisfactorily. My parents were very proud of me. We lived at a brisk pace; it was in December, we were organizing to go to the beach and she was preparing one of our favorite dishes to take along. She collapsed right there in front of our eyes. We took her to the hospital, they kept her and the series of testing began again .The results were not good. The doctor said that apparently the cancer had gone into recession after the operation but now it had resurfaced and it was very aggressive. In fact it had spread to her bones and organs. They began a series of chemotherapy treatment. Those were very bad days. My parents would go to the hospital on an evening and when they came back in the night my father would almost be carrying her. Those nights I would hear her vomiting violently but they would never let me enter. The door would be locked.

"Daddy, open the door, please," I'd plead. "Open the door. I'm a part of this just like you are. Sam, open the door now or I'll break it down."

But it was only after she felt better and had composed her-self that they would open the door and she would be sitting on the bed looking very normal and say, "Everything is okay, Tommy." She became a master at hiding her feelings, but as time went by whenever I wanted to get a true picture of her progress all I had to do was look at my father, because all her agony and hopelessness showed on his face.

She went downhill quickly. The doctor wanted to ward her at the hospital but there was no way that she was going to leave us. Whenever someone came to visit her it was difficult to distinguish patient from visitor. Somehow she always managed to be more cheerful than the people who visited her.

One morning, she said to me, "You see how my belly has swollen, Tommy? I think I'm making you another brother or sister."

I said, "Mummy, your eyes are turning yellow also."

She took up a little mirror that was at her bedside and looked into it. "My goodness."

The next morning she got up early and packed her bag.

"Samuel," she said, "I am ready to go to the hospital."

When we got there, they immediately hooked her up to oxy-gen and other apparatus.

My father and I went home around noon to put things in place, but by the time we got back she was already unconscious. We stayed with her through the night. She left us at two-thirty in the morning. My father and I were devastated. From the time of her death to the day of her funeral everything seemed like a blur. We lowered her coffin in an incessant rain.

When we got back to the empty house reality *re'lly* hit us. The threesome was broken. The strongest was taken away and all that was left were two weakened digits. I could remember my first year in college the teacher asked us to make one sentence to de-scribe our family. I wrote: *My family is like a rose.* Now that rose was no more, the petals had fallen off and left an uncertain future seed and a wilted stem. In the weeks that followed, I watched my father turn into a walking ghost and he might have been able to say quite the same about me. He would still set the table for three and he would sit there, barely picking at his food, and look at the extra plate as if to say, 'What's the matter, dear? Not going to eat your food tonight?' The colours of the rainbow had all turned to grey. The greenery of the trees, the multicoloured cars and houses, everything seemed grey to my eyes.

One night I was angry and wanted to confront God. I had to drink in order to do so. I found alcohol left over from the wake and drank myself into a stupor.

I said, "Listen, Big Man, why did you have to take her now? Couldn't you have given her a couple more years? Look at all the good things she had done for us and just as I was about to get a job so I could buy her nice things you went and took her away. Why, Man, why!" But then I realised that I was acting foolish. The Big Man was always kind, loving and just. Maybe he had seen her works. That's it. He had seen her works and sent her off to a better place. I got up and stumbled over to my father's room and opened the door.

I said, "Sam, you don't have to worry, boy, he has sent her off to a better place."

Sam rolled over. "What did you say, Tommy?"

"I said you don't have to worry, she's gone to a better place!"

The next morning I got up and tried to make his favorite breakfast: common fowl eggs fry up with saltfish, and fried bakes. I set the table for two and called out to him, "Breakfast is ready, your lordship, come and get it." He came to the table with an extra plate, teacup and saucer.

I said, "Take it back, man, there are only two of us here." He seemed reluctant. I said, "Remember what I told you last night, man? She's gone to a better place. You don't want to keep her back, do you?"

He returned the utensils to the cupboard and ate reasonably well.

"How about you take me fishing tomorrow, Sam?" I asked him after breakfast.

"Sounds like a good idea," he said.

The next day we went fishing off the coastal village of Moruga. We caught us a nice cavali, and that night Sam made one of his special fish broths. We enjoyed it.

Two days later, I said over breakfast, "It's four months since she died, Sam. The grave would have settled enough. It's time to build her a tomb."

"I will arrange for someone to get it done," he said.

"No, sir, she would have wanted us to build it with our own hands."

We bought bricks, cement and sand and in our own way, fashioned a reasonable structure. It took us two days. On the second day we purchased a pizza and took it along with us.

"You think she's looking at us?" asked Sam.

"Better than that," I said. "Knowing her she is probably helping us."

When we were finished, we sat around the tomb eating pizza and admiring our handy work.

"There is only one thing left to do," I said. "What should we mark on the headstone?"

Sam thought for a while and said, "'Herein *lies an Angel*'."

I said, "That sounds good, but something is missing."

"Well?" asked Sam.

"She was a very strong woman, Sam."

"How about '*Herein lies a Strong Angel*'?"

"That's it!" I said, and a genuine smile covered my father's face for the first time since the petals had fallen from the rose.

The Stranger

When we were small, my father told us some grand stories about his father, who was one of the original whalers on the tiny island of Bequia in the Grenadines. How he would go out in his little skiff and harpoon the whales that would sometimes drag him across the Caribbean Sea all the way to St. Lucia. How at night the Bequinians would light big bonfires on the hills overlooking the seashore to guide him home when he was late in coming. Naturally, when I left school at eighteen, though equipped for "better" vocation, I decided to become a fisherman.

When I was nineteen years old, the captain of the boat I worked on went off to work on a shrimp trawler and the owner of the boat asked me to take over the captaincy. I was elated. Her name was The Intruder. She was a twenty-seven-foot, wooden pirogue with an old forty horsepower Evinrude outboard engine. She was nothing more than an old wooden tub, but when I took her out that first morning, I felt as if I was taking out the Queen Mary, one of the largest ocean liners in those days. It's difficult to explain the thrill.

We were a crew of five: Santa Flora was a seasoned old salt with a big heart and a stomach to match—he was one of the most capable eaters on the waterfront; Gandy was the eldest amongst us—he was a good old sport that got better with every drink of rum that he took; Jupiter was not much older than I—he was a good seaman and a top class footballer; Sinbad The Sailor had just drifted into Icacos Village from Port of Spain about a month ago–he was yet an unknown quantity. It was the month of August and there was a good run of redfish on, and after two weeks we were beating the bigger boats with more experienced crews at the scales. My brothers said it was beginner's luck; my father said it was not so–he said that I was a natural sea dog, just like my grandfather. After three weeks the redfish eased up and we were scraping along with the other boats.

The Saturday of the fourth week we decided to make an early tide, since on that evening, Jupiter, who played for the Dynamos Football Club, was involved in a semi-final football match in the Cedros Football League. We went to sea at four in the morning and by eight o'clock all we had caught was one large Cavali about ten pounds. We decided to knock it off for the day. We would go in, prepare a meal of dumplings and stewed Cavali, and, since we all wanted to see Jupiter play, we would relax until it was time to go to the football match. While we were heading in, Santa Flora scraped the scales off from the Cavali and cut it into neat slices, placing them into a clean bucket that we had onboard. When we got in, we anchored The Intruder in shallow waters and, armed with our bucket of sliced Cavali, we retired to the ranch house where the crew stayed. Our ranch house was just a crude little hut on the beach that the owner of the boat had built to house his crew, and I lived not too far from it, but of late I found myself spending more time there than at home.

Santa Flora took out a large basin, filled it with flour, added some salt and water and proceeded to knead the dough for the dumplings; Gandy washed the Cavali slices with limes and water and seasoned it with his spices, while Jupiter and I went and gathered firewood from under the coconut trees. When we returned, we placed the firewood into the old fireside that stood in front the ranch house, while Sinbad The Sailor sat on the steps cutting his toe nails with an old rusty penknife. Santa Flora lit the firewood. Then he placed a pitch oil tin, half-filled with water, onto the fireside, and when the water began to boil he placed in his dumplings.

They were huge seamen dumplings that we called "cattle tongues" because they quite resembled a cow's tongue in size and shape. When the dumplings floated to the top of the boiling water, Santa Flora scooped them out with a large spoon, and into a basin, because their floating to the top was the sign that they were cooked. Then, using some old rags to shield his hands from the heat, he removed the pitch oil tin from the fireside. Gandy then came with his pot of Cavali and settled it on the fireside to stew. We sat around the fire, predicting the scores of the impending football match, with Santa Flora trying to coax Gandy into a wager, but Gandy telling him in no uncertain terms that his money was strictly for buying alcohol, not for placing bets. When the stew was finished cooking, each man went into the ranch house and came back with a bowl as large as he could find, and we sat around the fireside, its embers still glowing, partaking in the delicious meal; suddenly we noticed a stranger coming towards us.

He was well-dressed in a blue long-sleeved shirt and black long pants, and as he came closer, we noticed that he wore a worried look on a boyish face and an immaculate brown pair of *Clarks* desert boots. He stood a few feet from us and muttered something like good morning. Gandy got up, went into the hut, returned with an empty bowl, passed it to The Stranger and invited him to help himself. The Stranger declined and then casually announced:

'I going and kill myself.'

Santa Flora picked up a dumpling the size of his palm – one that would have easily choked an elephant – tucked it neatly into his mouth and still managed to grunt to The Stranger while he chewed:

'So... why... you ...want to kill yourself for?'

'My wife leave me and gone with the postman,' said The Stranger.

'Welcome to the club,' said Gandy whose wife had run off with a bus driver. 'But as you see, that is no reason to kill yourself.'
The Stranger pursed his lips and looked solemn.

'Plus,' Sinbad The Sailor added, 'any man who could afford to walk around in a pair of boots like what you have on there, ain't have no reason to kill himself.'

'You want them?' asked The Stranger, already undoing the laces.

'Want them? Man! Is years now I hoping to own a pair of boots like that! But I can't afford it.'

The Stranger, who by now had already finished undoing his laces, pulled off the boots and passed them to Sinbad. Sinbad placed his bowl of food on the ground, gleefully accepted the pair of boots from The Stranger, immediately stood, went into the hut, came back with his toothbrush and began brushing away the tiny particles of sand that had collected around the soles.

'Sit down and have something to eat with us, son, and forget about the woman,' coaxed Gandy.

Instead The Stranger began peeling off his clothes until he wore only his underwear. He passed the clothes to Sinbad.

'You can have these too,' he said. And he took off running towards the sea.

Instinctively, all of us placed our bowls of food on the sand and started running after him (all except Sinbad, of course, who was already trying on The Stranger's clothes to see if it would fit). By the time we got to the sea, he was already swimming off in long easy strokes, as if he was headed for the mainland of Venezuela, so instead of swimming out to him, we raced towards the boat, got in and while I started the engine, Jupiter ran up to the bow and weighed in the anchor. I engaged the forward gear and headed towards The Stranger. At this point he was already about one hundred yards out to sea. I brought The Intruder close to him. Jupiter, Gandy and Santa Flora were all on the bow of the vessel now. I neutralized the engine and the men began pleading with him to abandon his goal and come back to land with us, but The Stranger kept on swimming.

'Listen man! What is your plan?' Santa Flora shouted, and when The Stranger stopped swimming, I engaged forward again, getting closer to him, then I switched back to neutral.

Threading water, The Stranger said, 'My plan is to swim until I get so tired that I can't swim anymore, then I will give up the Ghost and allow myself to drown,' and he began lengthening off in those long easy strokes again. The sea was as calm as a lake and he was a fantastic swimmer. (If someone was observing us from the air, they would probably have thought that we were escorting a long distance swimmer on a record breaking run. They would never have guessed that we were trying to save this man's life.)

'Now why the hell would a woman want to leave a man who could swim like that to run off with a postman?' inquired Gandy.

'Beats the hell out of me,' responded Santa Flora.

Jupiter was looking up at the sun, trying to gauge the time. 'If this madman keep on swimming like that, at four o' clock this afternoon I'll be playing football in Venezuela instead of Cedros,' he protested.

I engaged the forward gear again and took The Intruder right up to him. He stopped swimming and the men tried another round of coaxing:

'Come on, boy, she ain't worth it and besides we haven't got all day,' said Jupiter impatiently.

'But what this world coming to? A man can't even drown himself in peace,' said The Stranger and he started to swim again.

We were now more than one nautical mile off the beach. Jupiter looked up at the sun again and spat into the water. The engine was still in neutral, and we all gathered in the centre of the boat.

'I say let we drive alongside the man, I'll jump overboard and put some good blows on him and we will tie him up and put him in the boat,' said Jupiter.

'Nah, boy, suppose something go wrong,' said Gandy. 'The next thing you know they charging all of us for murder.'

'Is true,' said Santa Flora, 'the law is a funny thing. That same girl that putting him through all this predicament will go in court and say is we that kill the man.'

We remained there discussing for a while. Santa Flora and Gandy were visibly losing their patience and Jupiter was furious, because the sun was beginning to lean towards the west and football was on his mind. A mild wind began blowing out of the north and little ripples began to appear on the surface of the water. Santa Flora said:

'Drive up to him one more time, *Cappie*, and let me try to reason with him,' and I engaged the engine and took The Intruder up to him; he stopped swimming.

'Listen, son, that girl ain't worth throwing your life away for,' pleaded Santa Flora. 'I'll tell you what. I have two nice daughters with a Spanish woman in Siparia. Come back with us and I'll take you up there and introduce you to them.'

Still threading water, The Stranger lifted his head and looked up at Santa Flora who was leaning over the bow of the pirogue.

'They resemble you?' he asked.

'Yes, yes,' said Santa Flora intensely.

'Well, I rather dead!' said The Stranger. And he broke into those long easy strokes of his again.

Santa Flora was visibly hurt; he looked like a priest who had been accused of stealing. I called for another meeting in the middle of the boat and the men gathered around.

'We really have to do something now. This boy playing the fool!' fumed Jupiter.

'Yes. And he getting disrespectful too,' said Santa Flora, maintaining a sort of hangdog look.

I suggested, 'Ok, gentlemen, let us each put forward a plan, and we will choose the best one and execute it.'

When all was put forth we agreed on Santa Flora's idea, and I engaged the engine into forward again. Santa Flora began loosing the anchor rope from the anchor. When he was finished, he took the end of the rope and tied a lasso. The Intruder covered a good distance before we met The Stranger again.

'This boy should be swimming in the Olympics instead of trying to drown himself,' commented Gandy.

We were now close to The Stranger. Santa Flora turned to me.

'Ok, Cappie, I just want you to get alongside him and leave the rest to me.'

In quick succession, I began shifting the engine from forward to neutral, because I did not want the propeller to draft him in. Santa Flora stood with his lasso in his hand, like a cowboy, as The Intruder got into position, and when The Stranger's right hand went up in that lovely stroke of his, out went Santa Flora's lasso and he expertly encircled The Stranger's neck and shoulder. Immediately Gandy and Jupiter held on to the rope and dragged The Stranger towards the gunwale. Then they yanked him into the boat. The Stranger was cursing vehemently as they flung him down. Jupiter jumped on him, sat on his chest and began cuffing him about the face.

'Oh God! Oh God! You go kill me!' shouted The Stranger.

'And is dead you want to dead? Take this in you mother arse,' said Jupiter, as he connected with a brutal right that drew a streak of blood from The Stranger's lower lip.

'Ok, Jupiter that is enough!' I shouted and Santa Flora held him.

The Stranger began to cry. Then he began to laugh.

'But I really stupid yes. Look how good I feeling now and I was just trying to kill myself,' he said, while he tried to get to his feet.

Jupiter grabbed him and held him in a bear hug. 'None of that bullshit! If you feel you going to jump out of this boat you lie!'

I looked at The Stranger and noticed that the worried look was gone from his face. Now he had an expression of relief. I realised that he had rediscovered his true self.

'I think he is ok now, Jupiter. You can release him,' I said.

'You sure, Cappie?' asked Jupiter.

I looked at The Stranger again and thought I was reading him right. 'Yes.'

Jupiter released him. The Stranger then began moving around the boat offering each one of us his heartfelt thanks. Gandy and Santa Flora hugged him, and Santa Flora told him that he was glad that he was okay now, because he seemed like a young fellow with a lot of potential. Meanwhile, I engaged the engine into forward and turned the boat towards Icacos. I began coaxing whatever speed I could get out of the old engine, because I knew that Jupiter was worried about missing his match. When we were almost in, The Stranger turned to me. 'You think that fellar will give me back my clothes and boots?'

'Don't worry over it,' I said.

When we got in, we anchored The Intruder safely and went up to the ranch house. Sinbad The Sailor was sitting on the step, still grooming the boots with that toothbrush of his; when he saw The Stranger he was clearly disappointed. Gandy went into the ranch and returned with the bowl that he had previously offered The Stranger. This time he took it and helped himself to some food. The bowls of food that we had left on the sand were still more or less in the same condition; except for the odd fly that had drowned in the stewed fish. These we carefully extricated with our spoons and then we dug in. We sat there like a band of brothers talking and laughing. The Stranger was absorbing the butt of most of our jokes but he laughed along with us all the same. When we were finished eating The Stranger turned to Sinbad, who was still sitting on the step grooming the boots, and said to him:

'Partner. I not asking you back for my things, but, I asking you to loan them to me, so I could get home, and I will bring them back for you in a couple of days.'

'Bring them back? Sure you will bring them back! Just like you was going to kill yourself.'

'Listen, you don't have to believe me, but my father have a big store on High Street. I swear that I will come back,' said The Stranger.

Reluctantly, Sinbad gave him back his clothes, but he took a hell of a long time in passing the boots. After, it turned out that The Stranger had no money to travel back home, so we 'passed the hat' between us and made up bus fare to get him there. Sinbad refused to put in any.

'How come a man who say he father own a big time store, ain't have passage to go back home?' he asked.

'How many men you know, who set out to kill themselves, would walk with money to travel back home?' I asked him.

He *steupsed* and walked away.

The Stranger left us, completely at ease with himself, and we were happy to see him go like this. Jupiter was already bathing from a barrel of rain water at the side of the hut, courtesy a bamboo spouting that we had installed on the edge of the roof. Gandy, Santa Flora and myself were just lying there in the sand waiting our turn to bathe and Sinbad was sulking on the step.

'What I can't understand,' he said, 'is why the hell all you had to run out there, play hero and save that stupid boy.'

Santa Flora got up. I could see the anger in his eyes and I should have gotten up too, but it seemed that those dumplings had anchored me to the ground. He went straight up to Sinbad.

'So you would of preferred for that promising young man to kill himself, so you could get his boots?'

'If he so stupid, I doh have a problem with that,' said Sinbad. 'Look! All you doh even know he name.'

I saw those big, thick fingers of Santa Flora folding in on his right hand and forming into a fist. I forced myself up now, but already I knew that I was too late; that huge right fist of Santa Flora connected with the side of Sinbad's face and sent him sprawling off the steps and onto the ground. The area around the ranch house got unusually quiet. I could hear the little waves churned up by the gentle north wind washing against the shore. Sinbad raised himself up using his elbow. He didn't say a word. He just walked up the two steps, went into the ranch and came back out with his bag. I was afraid that he was going to leave us, but then he sat down on the step for what seemed like an eternity. We were all looking at him; even Jupiter, who, on hearing the commotion, had abandoned his bath, stood there with his mouth slightly opened, his body white with soap, his eyelids trying to blink off some lather that was getting into his eyes. Then Sinbad got up. He went back into the ranch, hung his bag on the nail where it was before and he came out and said:

'Gentlemen. I'm sorry. I guess I let that pair of *Clarks* get the better of me.'

Immediately I could see relief on their faces.

We bathe, got ourselves ready and all of us went to the football match. Dynamos won the match, two goals to one, with Jupiter scoring the first item.

A few weeks later, around four in the afternoon, we were at the side of the ranch house playing a game of cards. There we were, standing around our makeshift table, which was merely an empty barrel with a square piece of ply board on the top, when a sleek-looking red car pulled up at the end of the road. From where we were, we could see that the chauffeur was a girl. Someone came out of the front passenger seat. It was The Stranger.

When he got out, he opened the back door of the vehicle and took out a large black bag, and he came towards us with it. He greeted us with a great deal of excitement and showered us with gifts from the black bag. Last of all, out came the boots from the bag. Sinbad smiled from ear to ear and accepted it.

'Like you make back with the *wifey*?' asked Santa Flora, pointing to the girl in the car.

'Nah, man, that is a new girlfriend I pick up,' said The Stranger.

'But you is a real quick mover,' said Gandy. The Stranger blushed.

Sinbad stood there admiring the boots and then he turned to The Stranger.

'When you see that girl in the car there start giving you trouble, make sure and buy a new pair of this, black if you please, put it on your foot and then you could come back down here to attempt your *stupidness*.'

I could see the anger creeping into Santa Flora's eyes, and immediately I got between him and Sinbad. But Santa Flora restrained himself and started to laugh. We all started to laugh.

Is he young or is he old?

If it have a heaven on earth it sure to be Trident Base. This off-shore oil company have their headquarters on the south western peninsula of Trinidad. Man, the place is a real paradise. One Company One People; that is the motto. And is true, workers and management living like one big happy family in there. The only problem is when is time to resign, the place so nice nobody want to leave.

So when personnel calls in Mr. So-and-so or Ms. So-and-so and say, you know, you have only one more year to go to retirement, right away that person does start to put up a defence, saying that it have some mistake, because they sure they still have a couple of years to go. The next day when you see that person, you can't make them out. They dye their hair in the prettiest black you could ever see. They should give the people that making that dye the Nobel Prize for Chemistry. A few weeks later, that same person would waltz into personnel with a birth paper that they borrow from their younger brother or sister from Grenada or St. Vincent, and they arguing with personnel that they did make a mistake with the spelling of their first name on their date of employment. The people in personnel so nice, they say, hold on, we going to check on the old files in the back, but when they get there they can't find it, because the rats ate it a long time ago. So they come back and say, Mr. So-and-so or Ms. So-and-so, it is possible that we *might* have made a

85

mistake, and the next thing you know that person making a couple extra years, depending on the age of the person who furnished the birth paper. The Trident people aware of these proverbial dinosaurs that walking around in the system; they does call them the 'first-name-spelt-wrong-younger-relative-birth-paper scammers.'

It have one they call Melvin Tourist, his hair black like jet but everybody say he on the other side of seventy. The man have a golden smile; when he open his mouth gold teeth park up in there like new car in Neal and Massy showcase. One day Melvin was working on Platform B and he fall in the sea. The dye from Melvin's hair turn the whole sea black. The safety officer didn't see anybody fall in the sea, but when he look out, he see the black water. He radioed the base:

'Trident Base, Trident Base, come in to Platform B, over.'

'Trident Base, receiving, come in, over.'

'There is an oil spill around Platform B. Send down some cansorb, over.'

'How many bags? Over.'

'Bags? Boy, the whole sea black, you better send a boat load!'

'Sending cansorb right away, over.'

It had a contractor fellar on the lower deck that see when Melvin fall in. He rushed up the stairs and alerted the safety officer. The safety officer dropped the transmitter, raced downstairs and threw a life ring into the water, then he and the contractor worker began looking for signs of Melvin. Lucky for Melvin the current was pushing under the platform and he managed to grab hold of a beam. The safety officer saw him clutching on for dear life and pointed him out.

'Nah, that is not the man,' said the contractor worker, 'his hair was different.'

'I is the same man that fall in,' Melvin shivered. 'Why the two of you don't hush all y'u tail and get me out of this blasted water?'

The boatload of cansorb arrived after they pull Melvin out the water.

One day, Melvin cruisin' through Point Fortin and he bounce up this nice young lady in front of First Citizens Bank. Right away Melvin pelt a tackle. The young lady looking at Melvin's beautiful, black hair, ain't realise is a geriatric she dealing with, take the bait. Things start to get cozy between the two and one day the young lady just ups and ask Melvin to take her to the beach. Melvin get on the defensive right away, but the young lady insist, so he picked her up and they gone down Clifton Hill. They sat on the sandy beach for a while and suddenly the girl got up and went to the change room to put on her bath suit. Immediately, Melvin start to think up excuse because he know sea water and dye don't mix. Same time, some killer bees passed by looking for a place to nest, see Melvin's beautiful, black hair. Melvin hear "zoom, zoom," and when he look up he see the bees about to swarm him. Melvin get frighten, dashed for the sea and dive in the water. The killer bees dispersed but all Melvin's hair was white now. He came out of the water the same time the lady returned in her exotic two-piece bikini.

'Mister,' she asked, 'you see the man I was sitting here with a while ago?'

'But eh-eh, babes, you ain't make me out?' Melvin placed his hands on the girl's shoulders. 'Is me, honey.'

'Listen, mister, get y'u' blasted perverted hands off me, I didn't come down here with no old man.'

It have another 'birth-paper scammer' they call Beresford. He take the cake. Old age pleat up the man's face like if a backhoe dig trench on it. Yet he hair blacker than coals. You remember it had a horse named Black Beauty? Well Black Beauty's mane was a joke next to Beresford's. When the Mighty Duke sang *Black is Beautiful* it had to be Beresford's hair that inspired him. One day Beresford and a fellar named Natty was working urgently on a fire pump, out in the open, on Platform D. Natty working but he admiring Beresford's black hair. All of a sudden the rain start to fall and Beresford's hair begin to turn white. Natty say:

'Mr. Beresford, like you related to the bullfinch or what?'

'Natty, why you don't hush you mouth? You ever hear man and bird does be related?'

'Well they must be,' Natty laughed, 'because I stand up right here and I see your hair molting from black to white. And is only birds does moulter!'

Beresford start to cuss.

He came with his hair jet black the next day.

Signs of advanced old age start to manifest itself all over Beresford's physical being. Except his hair. He start coming to work with a walking stick, and if the sea was rough, in the evening he going back home in a wheelchair.

The safety department was worried about Beresford's welfare. They gone to personnel, but personnel can't do nothing. Their hands tied; according to their files Beresford is only sixty three—a whole two years to go to retirement.

The person most affected by these proverbial dinosaurs was the Trident Base doctor, a fellar they call *The King of Pop*. Early every morning they in his office: they want something for the arthritis; something for back pain; and some of them so fresh up, they asking for the blue tablet to raise The Dead. The King of Pop was furious because they were wasting precious time, time that he could spend with more worthy patients.

One day The King of Pop was browsing a medical journal when something caught his attention: in China, they could tell a person's age by testing a lock of their hair. The King of Pop got excited. Finally, he could rid Trident Base of the proverbial dinosaurs. He called up the Trident Base Big Boss, Bobcolm Bones. Mr. Bones gave him the all clear. The King of Pop was overjoyed. He would start with Beresford.

When Beresford came in for his monthly checkup The King of Pop was waiting. Beresford was sitting in the nice reclining chair and The King of Pop was taking his pressure, when, softly, Beresford nodded off. Quietly, The King of Pop sneaked a scissors from his coat pocket, and began moving towards Beresford's black hair; Beresford's eyes sprang open.

'What the ass you going to do with that scissors?' he demanded.

The King of pop jumped back. 'Well... I saw a loose shock of hair that wasn't compatible with your hairstyle, so I thought that I would remove it.'

'As far as I know,' Beresford shouted, 'you is a doctor, not a barber. Leave my blasted hair alone!'

Now The King of Pop was a determined fellow, and a smart one too. He open the office door, walk into the corridor and he spoke to one of the lovely young nurses standing there, telling her exactly what he wanted and giving her the scissors. *Nursey* went into the office by herself and pretend to be retaking Beresford's pressure, all the while sweet-talking and caressing him, and Beresford rock back there, smiling in the recliner and pondering the possibility of asking The King of Pop for one of the blue tablets, when Nursey snipped off a lock and placed it in her pocket. As soon as The King of Pop got the hair it was express mail straight to China.

Six weeks later the results came back. Beresford was eighty three years. The King of Pop smiled. Finally he had him! But Big Boss Bobcolm Bones said he still needed more evidence.

The doctor hired a private eye. The detective uncovered that Trident's "Beresford" was really Telesford. Beresford was really a younger brother, twenty years Telesford's junior. When Trident sent Telesford, that birth-paper scammer, off on retirement, because of his long service, he received the biggest payoff ever. All the workers hoped that he would live long enough to spend all that big money.

The King of Pop continued pursuing the other 'first-name-spelt-wrong-younger-relative-birth-paper-scammers.' Express mail to China got busy; so did the private eye.

To cover the loop hole in the system, the Trident Base Big Boss, Mr. Bobcolm Bones, passed a decree: from now on, he said, any new worker joining the Trident Family will have to write their first name three times in capital letters followed by their signature. He made it clear that he was running an oil field, not a geriatric home.

He should know because it rumored that he an all long overdue. By at least nineteen years. They also say that his real name is Malcolm–Bobcolm is his younger brother that living in Grenada. It is also a known fact that whenever he is going for his monthly checkup by The King of Pop, he buys a razorblade and shaves his head clean like a whistle; old fox that he is. He knows that it is quite easy for a man his age to doze off in The King of Pop's comfy reclining chair and he suspects that the doctor is after him. So Mr. Bones is making no bones about it. He just can't afford to let his locks end up in express mail to China!

Raid across the border

Simon Gibson joined the Coastal Patrol Forces at age seventeen and quickly acquired a reputation. He was a restless mass of energy, never properly dressed, always barefooted, forever up to mischief, and was soon nicknamed 'The Pest'. He was from Erin, a fishing village. He climbed like a monkey, swam like a shark and though small of stature, stood up to the biggest men on the base and took them down a notch or two. Many officers thought he would be better off elsewhere, but there was one man keeping a sharp eye on The Pest.

Lieutenant Jack Fleary was in charge of the ECU (Elite Coastal Unit), a crack group comprising fifty of the best fighting men in the Coastal Patrol Forces (CPF). They went out when things got nasty: hijackings, hostage taking, rescue at sea in adverse conditions. Lt. Fleary handpicked these men. Fleary concluded that The Pest had the makings and knew he could mould him into something special.

Lt. Fleary was an English-schooled officer. During his overseas training gunmen killed his only sister. On that fateful day she had gone to the bank to drop off a key for their mother who worked as a teller. A robbery was in progress. The bank guards handled it badly and when the smoke cleared, three bandits, a guard and Jack Fleary's sister were dead. Fleary flew in for the funeral and returned to his training more determined. He topped his class, consisting of midshipmen from around the world. One year after Fleary returned to Trinidad, they put him in charge of the ECU. Fleary restructured the ECU, sending his men abroad to specialise in specific arts of warfare and exposing them to modern devices and technology. Meanwhile he successfully lobbied the Coastal Patrol Forces into purchasing new equipment. Fleary lived and breathed ECU and now had the licence to tackle the *real* bad guys.

Every CPF member dreamed of qualifying for the ECU. Scores of applications went in each year for the five or six available positions. When Fleary and his team received the applications, they started an elimination process until they got the applicants down to about twenty. Then he started a rigorous training programme in swimming, climbing, rappelling, intelligence gathering, boat handling, and shooting weapons of every calibre. After two months Fleary scooped up the five or six men he needed from this twenty then trained them alongside his ECU specialists. For the next six months they were schooled in different types of warfare. Later they were sent abroad to one of the finest fighting forces in the world for another three months to specialise in whatever field they chose: intelligence gathering, boat handling, room clearing, assault team leadership. Now full-fledged ECU men, Fleary sent them into the field. They were versatile and some even specialised in as many as four disciplines.

Fleary took special interest in The Pest because he saw in him characteristics of a complete warrior. He encouraged The Pest to enlist. "The ECU is like a spear," he told him, "and I see steel in you. I can make you into the perfect tip." The Pest enlisted and increased his edge. Fleary fine-tuned and sent him abroad on training stints. When The Pest graduated he became, at nineteen years and a day, the youngest member of the ECU. One year later, The Pest married his childhood sweetheart, Elizabeth, and had four children, the eldest a girl, and three boys. During this time, The Pest spearheaded many ECU operations, and even Fleary marvelled at his prodigy.

Friday, 25 Sep 1998, Erin Village, 1745 hours/ 05:45 PM

In the coastal village of Erin, behind a stack of lumber, stored across the road from a hardware, a contraband transaction between Venezuelans and a Trinidadian is in progress. Two police officers on a routine patrol stumble upon the deal and the Venezuelans, hostile, armed and dangerous, go into action. Under fire, the policemen dart behind the hardware and return the bitter compliment, but both parties are well-positioned, so it's merely a case of flying bullets.

The shooting stops, each side assessing the other. Along comes a grey car driven by Elizabeth Gibson, with her fifteen-year-old daughter, Ayana, in the front seat, and her three mischievous boys having a go at each other in the back. Elizabeth, not knowing she is in the calm of a siege, stops the car in front the hardware, with the intention of going in to purchase a gallon of paint before the store closes. The car is directly between the combatants.

The contrabandists run out from behind the lumber, open the front passenger door, grab Ayana and, using her as a shield, retreat to the beach. They bundle Ayana into the boat and speed off into the gathering darkness. In the midst of the excitement, their Trinidadian counterpart, a man the officers recognise as Pompey, escapes into the nearby bushes, leaving Mrs. Gibson and the policemen in disarray.

ECU Headquarters, Port of Spain, 1820 hours/ 06:20 PM

Lt. Fleary and one of his ECU men, James Parker, an expert room-clearer, codenamed The Hawk, are having a cheerful conversation. The phone rings and Lt. Fleary picks up the receiver. The Hawk watches closely as the Lieutenant's face takes on a solemn look. Fleary takes a pen and notebook out of his pocket and jots notes and, with the receiver still to his ear, turns to The Hawk and says:

'Get The Pest... now!'

The Pest is in the recreation room, playing cards with three other ECU men.

'The boss wants to see you,' The Hawk signals. The Pest hurries to the operation's room.

Within twenty minutes a chopper with Lt. Fleary, The Pest, The Hawk and three other heavily-armed ECU men is streaking across the Gulf of Paria to Erin. Meanwhile two four-wheel drive pickups from a Coastal Patrol Forces support unit stationed in Point Fortin, race towards Erin Beach, courtesy a phone call from Lt. Fleary placed five minutes before he boarded the chopper.

Erin Beach, 1900 hours / 07:00 PM

The helicopter lands at Erin Beach. The ECU team learns from witnesses and fishermen gathered around that the abductors have escaped across the border to Venezuela. Six minutes later the pickups arrive at Erin Beach and Fleary dispatches the chopper back to base. Fleary sent the two drivers, normal Coastal Patrol Officers, and The Pest in one of the pickups to The Pest's home, while the ECU team took the second pickup. The team consists of Fleary, The Hawk and the three heavily-armed ECU men. These three men are: Harvey Richards, codenamed The Thinker, an assault team leader and expert room-clearer; Jake Goddard, codenamed The Bear, the dray horse of the ECU and an expert room-clearer, big and strong, with the mobility of a smaller man; Bagwat Gayadeen, codenamed The Iguana, an intelligence officer and professional sniper.

The pickup carrying The Pest reaches his home; Elizabeth Gibson rushes into her husband's arms.

'Oh Lord, Simon,' she sobs, 'they gone with Ayana.'

'Don't worry, dear,' The Pest says, 'we will get her back.' They go into the boys' room where their three sons lie staring at the walls. They jump on their father and begin crying.

'Did you boys eat?' he asks.

'They haven't eaten since,' Mrs. Gibson says, still sobbing.

'Come, let me rustle up your favourite: hot dogs!' He led his family to the kitchen.

Meanwhile, the ECU team pays the Erin Police Station a business call. One of the policemen involved in the fracas passes on all the information to the team; The Iguana, his notebook in hand, records everything. With the interview terminated, the team boards the pickup and races to The Pest's home. After greetings and sympathetic gestures, Fleary requests a safe room where they could hold a briefing. A bedroom in the house is cleared of all personnel, and the team, together with Mrs. Gibson, occupies it behind closed doors. The Iguana takes a statement from Mrs. Gibson and she is excused from the room. The Iguana passes the notebook to Fleary who peruses it and says:

'From police intelligence we can assume the contrabandists headed towards Venezuela, but the no-good Trinidadian escaped into the bushes. The police know him as Pompey. Our best chance is to get Pompey; he might know where the girl was taken.'

'I can id Pompey,' The Pest says. 'I have seen him hanging out on the beach with a fisherman named Manny.'

'Do you know where this Manny lives?' Fleary asks.

'He lives in a hut on the beach.'

Fleary looks through the bedroom window and nods. 'Is there anything like an abandoned house in a secluded area around here?'

'My uncle has a wooden hut in an abandoned quarry down Buenos Ayres side,' The Pest replies, 'about two miles from here.'

'Any neighbours close by?'

'No. It's in a track, five minutes drive off the main road.'

'Perfect. Can we have access to it?'

'Sure. The hut is abandoned anyway.'

Fleary looks around at his men and says, casually, 'Okay, let's pay Manny a visit.'

The ECU team's pickup heads to the beach. The Pest points out Manny's hut. While The Hawk remains in the pickup, quickly and quietly, the others went into action. There is a front door, back door and side window to the hut. The Bear and The Thinker went to the back door; The Iguana covers the side window, and Fleary and The Pest rap forcefully on the front door. Manny bolts through the back door, a long marijuana cigarette in his mouth, straight into the path of The Bear who brings him down with a football tackle.

'Jesus, officer, is only a lil weed I smoking. I didn't do anything,' pleads Manny as The Bear pins him to the ground and Fleary slips on the handcuffs.

'Get that shit out of your mouth,' The Bear demands, clouting Manny behind his head so hard that the broken marijuana joint flew out of his mouth.

'Okay, Manny, do you have big fish hooks?' Fleary asks.

'Yes-boss-yes-boss, inside the hut.'

'Let's see what you've got,' Fleary says.

They enter the hut. Manny, with his hands pinned behind him, points with his foot to a box of fishing tackles in the corner.

'Very impressive, Manny,' Fleary says, rummaging through the box and finding two large fish hooks and a reel of nylon that could tackle a two-hundred-pound fish. Manny is sweating. 'Now, Manny, we are going to take a ride. I want no commotion whatsoever.'

'Okay, boss, nothing like commotion from me!'

They bundle him into the backseat and drove off, swinging left onto the main road and heading towards Buenos Ayres. A mile and a half later they turn right onto a red stone track leading to the abandoned quarry. In less than five minutes they arrive at The Pest's uncle's abandoned hut. They park next to the building, manhandle Manny out of the backseat, fling him in the tray and the entire team surrounds him.

'Oh God, all y'u please, don't kill me.'

'That depends on what you tell us,' says Fleary.

'Anything you want to know, boss, anything.'

'Where can we find Pompey?' asks Fleary.

Manny is silent. Fleary's fist connects with his face.

'Oh God, boss, I trying to think where to locate the man. You didn't have to lash me.'

'Okay, Manny, my apologies, you have one minute to think this over,' warns Fleary.

'It have a trace after you pass Buenos Ayres called Jackson Trace. Pompey have a hut about two hundred yards up inside. When the pace hot he does go in there and hide up.'

'Right side of the trace or left side?' asks Fleary.

'Right side,' says Manny.

'Is the hut alongside the road or far from the road?'

'Bout fifty feet off the road.'

'Are there any other houses on this road, Manny?'

'No, boss, none.'

'Okay, Manny, hope that Pompey is in his hut, or else—'

'Please, boss, go easy on me nah, ah tell you everything I know, I swear.'

'Okay, boys,' Fleary says, 'take him about twenty feet into the bushes behind the house and gag him. The Hawk will keep him company until we return.'

The Iguana and The Hawk escort their grumbling detainee, make him sit with his back against a tree trunk and The Hawk shoves a handkerchief in Manny's mouth. The Iguana rejoins the team. Meanwhile Fleary, with his flashlight, inspects the hut, joins the team and heads out in the pickup. Back on the main road The Pest speeds westward, stops about fifty feet before Jackson Trace and turns off the headlights.

'Okay, men,' says Fleary, 'we'll hug the trees until we get close to the hut, then The Thinker and Iguana would scout for doors and windows and report back.'

The Thinker and The Iguana creep in and circle the hut. When they get back The Thinker whispers to Fleary:

'Back door, front door, two windows.'

'Okay, The Bear takes the back door, The Iguana the right window, The Thinker the left, and The Pest and I will kick in the front door.'

Stealthily, they creep into position. A lamp lights the hut. Pompey lies in a hammock, picking his teeth with a matchstick. With the arranged signal The Pest and Fleary kick in the door. Pompey jumps and dashes for the back. The Pest grabs Pompey, even before he gets to the door, and places a Gurka knife to his throat. Fleary handcuffs him. After The Pest runs to the pickup and drives into Jackson Trace, Fleary blows out the lamp and takes it along with Pompey, whom they bundle inside the van. The van speeds off. At the abandoned quarry they swing into the track and drive slowly up to the lonely hut. Fleary gets out, lights the lamp and enters the building. He hangs the lamp on a nail.

'Bring in the prisoner!' he says.

The team comes up the two wooden steps, pushing Pompey.

Fleary snarls: 'Listen, Pompey, you could make this easy on yourself or you can make it hard. Were you part of the commotion near the Erin hardware this afternoon?'

Pompey doesn't answer – Fleary slaps him on his ear and he drifts across the room.

'I want to talk to a lawyer!' Pompey demands.

'Hear that boys? He wants to talk to a lawyer, and he's so damn lucky that we have one present... Big Bear!'

'Yes sir!' growls The Bear.

'Are you willing to represent this client?'

'Yes sir!' The Bear is measuring nylon. He cuts two pieces, about twenty feet long, and ties a hook to each end. The Iguana climbs onto The Bear's shoulders, pulls each line over a wooden rafter, and lowers the ends to The Bear.

'Are you ready to represent this man?' Fleary asks.

'Yes sir!' The Bear grunts.

The Iguana climbs down, grabs Pompey (who still has his hands handcuffed behind his back) and holds him in a bear hug. Pompey screams when The Bear pierces his right ear with a fish hook. With The Iguana still holding him, The Bear pierces Pompey's left ear with the other hook.

'Be quiet!' Fleary barks.

Pompey stifles a cry as blood trickles down his ears. The Bear pulls on the lines and the rafter groans under Pompey's weight.

'I am your lawyer,' The Bear says to a weeping Pompey. 'You have the right to remain silent, but then I will pull your ass to the roof to make you talk, so spill your guts and save yourself the misery.'

'Okay... I ask again.' Fleary glares at Pompey. 'Were you part of the fracas this afternoon in front of the hardware?'

The Iguana has his notebook and pen ready. Pompey is silent. The Bear pulls on the lines and Pompey's ears are stretched to their limit.

'Yes-yes-yes!' he cries; The Bear slackens the lines. The Iguana is writing.

'Do you know where they are taking the girl?' asks Fleary and The Bear tugs on the lines again.

'Please-please-please slacken the lines and I will tell you everything you want to know.'

'Okay, Bear, cut it a little,' Fleary says. 'Do you know where they are taking the girl?'

'They have a hideout on Ghost River, a trib'tary off the Macareo River in Venezuela. I feel they taking her there.'

'How far up the Macareo is this tributary?' asks Fleary.

'About twenty miles up,' Pompey says, looking at The Iguana who is scribbling. 'Is the first trib'tary on the right after you pass Wapowa, tha' is the Warahoon village.'

'Tell us where on Ghost River the hideout is situated,' says Fleary.

'When you enter Ghost River go up bout three-quarter mile and you go come to a bend in the trib'tary. 'Bout one hundred yards after tha bend is the hideout.'

'Is it a right bend or left bend?' asks Fleary.

'A right bend.'

'What side of the tributary is the hideout?'

'Left side.'

'Have you ever been to this hideout?'

'Yes.'

'How many times?'

'Several times.'

'How many men are usually at the hideout?'

'Around twelve.'

'Who bosses the outfit?'

Pompey is silent; The Bear tugs on the lines, Pompey is up on his toes, he winces, but still doesn't talk.

'Drag his ass to the rafter,' commands Fleary and The Bear yanks on the line.

'El Cuchillo! El Cuchillo!' Pompey screams, and The Bear releases the tension.

Shaking his head, Fleary says, 'That would be his alias. I want his correct name!'

Pompey is silent; The Bear, like a puppet master, brings him to his toes again; still silence. Fleary wipes his mouth, exhales, and punches Pompey in the gut, a dull, ugly sound. Pompey vomits a soupy mixture of fried fish, bake and cocoa tea. Rolling his eyes, he mutters:

'Antonio Vargas… Antonio Vargas.'

The Bear slackens the lines and Pompey slumps to the floor. Pompey shakes his head and looks around wildly. The Bear dips into his pocket, extracts a handkerchief and passes it to Fleary who swipes vomit off his shoes. When Fleary goes outside The Pest follows.

'I know the Macareo River all the way up to Wapowa Village, sir, I've been up it a couple times in my youth.'

'That would be very useful for what I have in mind,' Fleary says, as he speed dials the ECU Operations Centre.

Donald Simmons answers the phone. Fleary asks him to have the systems analyst run a trace on Antonio Vargas, alias El Cuchillo, and call him ASAP. He and The Pest reenter the hut. Pompey is on his knees as if praying. The ECU team mills around. Fleary says he is going back out to have a smoke. Wild-eyed, Pompey pleads, 'I could ge a smoke too, boss?'

Fleary signals to The Bear, 'What do you think, attorney? Does your client deserve a smoke?'

'I'd say yes to that, boss,' The Bear smirks.

Fleary lights a cigarette and places it between Pompey's lips. Pompey draws heavily on the cigarette. Using his thumb and index finger, Fleary removes the cigarette from Pompey's mouth; Pompey exhales with a sigh of relief. Patiently, Fleary repeats the process until the cigarette finishes.

'Let him relax a little,' Fleary says, jerking his thumb towards Pompey.

Fleary walks outside, removes his ski mask, lights a cigarette and draws sharply on it, the red glow at the end illuminating his face. He takes a few more pulls, drops the butt and crushes it with his boot. His phone rings. It is Donald Simmons with the information: Antonio Vargas, alias El Cuchillo, was a drug transporter, with Colombian ties, operating out of the Orinoco Delta with links to human trafficking. Fleary rocks back and exhales: the girl might still be alive. Once they dealt in human trafficking, a fifteen-year-old girl in good health was money in the bank. His earlier fears were allayed, but time was of the essence. Fleary scratches his chin and begins to calculate: the authorities would never sanction a raid on foreign soil. They'd refer it to their Venezuelan counterpart, and it would take days for them to move. Their only chance was a lightning raid across the border.

Fleary lights another cigarette and his thoughts roll back: he thinks of his own sister then his thoughts shift to The Pest who had become more like a little brother to him. He could remember the restless, prank-loving, little bastard, but he had spotted his potential and given him the opportunity. That investment had paid off because The Pest was now his front man. Fleary blew out a cloud of smoke. He would not stand idly by while punks made off with the daughter of a man who had risked his life for his country for seventeen years. Fleary thinks: damn the crooks; a big surprise awaited them. But Fleary knew the intricacies and liabilities of a covert operation, especially if things went wrong. To hell with it. He was going to throw caution to the wind. When the butt end of the cigarette burns his fingers, he drops and extinguishes it. He walks to the door, calls softly to The Pest, and they walk into the open. The Pest removes his ski mask and wipes his forehead.

'I think Ayana is alive,' Fleary says. He scratches a match – the glare reveals a sombre look on The Pest's face – and lights another cigarette. 'El Cuchillo has human trafficking links. I believe we should have The Thinker with us for the rest of what I have to say.' The Pest summons The Thinker.

'Gentlemen,' Fleary says, 'El Cuchillo traffics flesh. Alive, Ayana is a valuable asset. To save her we must act now... with or without permission. The abductors aren't aware of the information we have. I think they will take the girl to the hideout until they have a buyer.'

'But,' he continues, 'a twenty-four-foot Jet Drive Zodiac, with a machinegun mounted at the stern, an arsenal of weapons, a team of eight, and a lightning raid tomorrow night *could* stop that sale. It's our only chance.' In the darkness Fleary could sense the growing excitement of the two warriors. 'Let's go talk to Pompey about the hideout.'

Back inside, The Bear tugs on the lines, hauling Pompey the puppet to his feet. The Iguana opens his notebook. Walking around Pompey, Fleary continues:

'You mentioned visiting this hideout on several occasions... tell us what we should know.'

The Bear tugs; Pompey bawls, 'Oh-gorm-oh-gorm, it have two buildings.'

'These buildings, are they on the river bank or on stilts in the river?'

'Part on the river, part on the bank.'

Fleary stops in front Pompey. 'Please explain.'

'Listen, boss, tell you partner to slacken the lines. I give up. I will tell you anything you want to know, just slacken the lines.'

In the lamp's glow Fleary studies Pompey. He nods at The Bear, The Bear slackens the lines and Pompey says, 'Thank-you-father-thank-you-father.'

'We're waiting,' Fleary warns.

'The back o' the buildings flat on the river bank,' Pompey squeals. 'The front on stilts in the river, you know nah, pound down in the mud.'

'Size and description?' asks Fleary.

'The one on the left 'bout fifteen by twenty. The other one 'bout fifteen by thirty.'

Fleary looks at The Iguana sketching a ground floor plan. Fleary nods. 'How many rooms in the buildings?'

'No rooms. Each building just one big open space.'

'How far apart are the two buildings?'

'Bout twenty feet,' Pompey replies.

'Are the two buildings connected in any way?'

'Yeah. They connected at the front by a wooden walkway on stilts.'

Fleary waits until The Iguana stops sketching. 'Does their boat tie up on this wooden walkway?'

'No. In the middle of the walkway it have a wooden jetty jutting out in the river. They does tie the boat on the jetty.'

Fleary has resumed walking around Pompey. 'How long is the jetty?'

'Bout forty feet.'

'How wide is the tributary at this point?'

'Tributary? Oh, you mean *trib'tary*. 'Bout one hundred and fifty feet.'

'Did you ever notice any other vessel moored against this jetty?'

'No, only the one that take 'way the girl.'

'Describe.'

'Twenty-seven-feet, green fibreglass pirogue.'

'Engines?'

'Two.'

'Sizes and make?'

'One hundred and fifteen horsepower, Yamaha.'

'Any other buildings on this tributary?'

'No, none.'

'You mentioned that the buildings also rest on the river bank. Do any doors open to the river bank?'

'Yes, a back door a building.'

'Are the hinges on these doors like the ones we have here?'

Pompey squints in the lamp's glow. 'Yes, I think so, normal hinges.'

'What's the terrain like?'

'Flipping mud and mangrove.'

'Are you familiar with guns?' asks Fleary. Pompey is silent, defensive so Fleary shrugs at The Bear.

'Yes-yes,' Pompey replies.

'You mentioned twelve men. What types of guns they carried?'

'AK47s, UZIs and Magnums.'

The Iguana nods at Fleary.

'Okay, Mr. Pompey, that will be all, for now. Gentlemen, take him out back with Manny. The Thinker, The Pest and I need to tie up some loose ends. Iguana, Bear, stand guard with The Hawk until we get back.'

'So is Manny, that *backstabber*, that tell you where to find me,' grumbles Pompey.

'Be quiet!' Fleary snaps, as he collects the notebook from The Iguana, thumbs through it and places it in his pocket. The Bear and The Iguana move Pompey, and Fleary blew out the lamp.

At The Gibson's home Fleary, The Thinker and The Pest set up shop in the bedroom. On a large sheet of paper supplied by Mrs. Gibson, Fleary sketches Trinidad's south coast. He makes a dot on the coastline and marks it as Galfa Point then he draws the Venezuelan coastline and leaves a space for the mouth of the Macareo River.

'Draw in the Macareo River up to Wapowa Village,' Fleary says to The Pest. After, Fleary spreads the sketch on the bed. Leaning over and tracing and pointing with his pen, he recalls: 'According to Pompey you travel about twenty miles up the Macareo until you come to Wapowa, a Warahoon Village. Another half mile up, on the right side, you come to Ghost River. Correct?' The men nod and Fleary sketches in the missing part. 'Good. Three-quarters of a mile up this tributary, there's a right bend and a hundred and fifty feet further, on the left bank, is the hideout.' The Pest and The Thinker nod. Fleary sketches in the hideout with its two buildings, walkway and jetty. 'There we have it, gentlemen, more than we could ask for.'

Someone knocks on the door. It is Mrs. Gibson's sister, Alana, with sandwiches and coffee. The refreshments went on the bed head. The Pest tells her to prepare takeaway sandwiches for five persons, and she exits. The Pest closes the door, the men refresh themselves and Fleary asks:

'Remember the training exercise on Galfa Point earlier this year?'

The Pest and The Thinker nod.

'That's just a couple of miles from here. We stage the raid from there. There is a back road that goes from Cedros straight to Galfa Point. Okay... you two... look closely at this.' Fleary holds up his sketch. 'We take off from Galfa Point across the sea to the Macareo, that's about eighteen miles. Another twenty from the river's mouth to Wapowa, then a half mile again to Ghost River. Three-quarter mile up is the hideout. That's thirty nine and a quarter miles, forty, give or take. The Jet Drive Zodiac gets sixty miles an hour. We go dead slow up Ghost River so they won't hear us then we paddle when we reach close to the bend. Give or take these two factors plus weather conditions, we could get to the hideout in seventy five minutes. We'll need four room-clearers, team leader included, a boat handler, a machine gunner, a sniper and a spotter.'

The Pest and Thinker nod.

'Time for the battle plans,' Fleary says.

They study the sketch closely, making tactical modifications regarding artillery and strategic positioning. With the plan hatched, Fleary says, 'Okay, men, logistics,' and passes the notebook and pen to The Thinker. When the list is completed Fleary looks at his watch. 'Good heavens, it's ten past midnight.' He dials Operations.

Donald Simmons, professional room-clearer and trained medic, codenamed The Dove, answers the phone. Fleary asks for Sub Lt. Julius Thompson, second in command of the ECU. A sleepy Thompson answers, 'What can I do for you, sir, at this glorious hour?'

'I have to admit, Thompson, it's quite an ungodly hour, but the situation dictates,' says Fleary. 'I have a list. Do you have pen and paper close by?'

Thompson sits at the desk and curses Fleary in his mind. 'Roger, sir.'

'We're going to need,' Fleary says, 'one 24-foot Jet Drive Zodiac, with a mounting for a general purpose machinegun at the stern; one general purpose machinegun with an extra barrel; four UZI submachine guns; two Parker Hale sniping rifles with scopes; eight Browning pistols; one twelve gauge shotgun; eight pairs of Night Vision Goggles; a map of the Macareo River; one pair binoculars; five magazines of GPMG ammunition (200 rounds each); forty fully-charged magazines of UZI submachine gun ammunition; fifty fully-charged magazines of Browning pistol ammunition; one hundred rounds of Parker Hale sniping rifle ammunition; one box twelve gauge cartridges; eight fully-charged torchlights; sixteen packets of MREs (Meals Ready-to-Eat); six paddles; four machetes; two large camouflage nets; one small camouflage net; six stun grenades; one dozen hand grenades; medical kit with standard battle supplies; large tarpaulin; eight Gurka knives; eight headsets.'

Thompson blurts: 'You planning on starting a war or something, sir?'

'Nope, just a routine island patrol, Thompson. Also I want you to send Simmons, Reifer, Sanchez and five more ECU men.'

'When do you want this stuff, sir?'

'ASAP. Outfit the Zodiac with a full capacity of fuel, pack in some of the equipment and let Reifer, Sanchez and two of the men sail her to Galfa Point. Contact me when they get there. The rest of equipment and an extra hundred gallons of fuel for the Zodiac go onto a large transporter truck. Let Simmons and the other three men man the truck. Simmons knows how to get to Galfa Point; he was on the training exercise with us earlier this year. Double check all the equipment before it leaves.'

'Okay, sir, anything else?'

'Throw in a couple sleeping bags, rations and water for a camp of sixteen men for two days.'

'Will do,' says Thompson.

'Call me as soon as you have a departure.'

'Will do, sir, over and out,' Thompson says.

Fleary turns to his men. 'Okay, gentlemen, we head back to the quarry then shift camp to Galfa Point.'

The Pest collects the sandwiches from his sister-in-law. He kisses his wife, and checks his sons, asleep in their bedroom. Meanwhile, Fleary has a word with the two CPF officers outside, instructing them to keep a lid on things at The Pest's home.

· At the quarry The Pest distributes sandwiches to the three ECU men and two prisoners. They take Pompey into the hut, light the lamp and interrogate him again. Fleary's phone rings. Thompson reports: 'We have a departure of both the Zodiac and The Transporter, sir.'

'Everything accounted for?'

'Yes, sir, everything checked and double-checked.'

'ETA for the Zodiac at Galfa Point?'

'Yes, sir, 0255 hours.'

'And The Transporter?'

'0410 hours.'

'Thank you very much, Mr. Thompson, we will be in contact.'

Fleary checks his watch: 0105 hours. He turns to his men. 'We'll take a short break now. Bring in the other prisoner and place him in that corner with Pompey. The Hawk and I will keep an eye on them. The rest of you, get some sleep while the stars are out.'

Fleary's spends his time killing mosquitoes and quieting Pompey who curses Manny bitterly. At 0205 hours Fleary croons: '*Wakey, wakey*, boys.'

The Iguana pushes himself up on his right elbow and wipes sleep from his eyes. The Pest, The Thinker and The Bear are already sitting.

'We head for Galfa Point immediately,' Fleary says.

The Pest is driving, Fleary is in the front passenger seat and The Thinker and Iguana are in the backseat. Pompey sits between them. Manny is in the tray with The Bear and The Hawk. They pass through the village of Buenos Ayres, down to Cap-de-Ville junction and swing left, onto the road leading to Cedros. The pickup is covering ground quickly: through the village of Chatham, down to the village of Coromandel; they are in Cedros; they swing left to the old Cedros Hospital and come upon the Galfa Road; down the lonely road they go, all the way to the beach. The Pest pulls up fifty feet from the water's edge. Fleary's watch says 0246 hours. He comes out of the pickup and stretches his legs on the beach. The Pest joins him.

'Zodiac should be here shortly,' says Fleary. The Pest is silent. Fleary's phone rings. It's Reifer, a spotter, codenamed The Squirrel.

'We are five minutes from destination, sir,' says Reifer.

'Okay, Squirrel, we are already on location awaiting your arrival. I will give you two blinks of the pickup's light and you'd drop off Sanchez onshore. Then you and the other two men would take the Zodiac back out and lay at anchor until morning.'

'Will do, sir.' The Squirrel hangs up.

Fleary and The Pest go back to the pickup and wait. They hear the Zodiac approaching. Out at sea, a red port light comes into view, then, against the backdrop of night, a silvery spray at the bow. Fleary reaches into the pickup and blinks the headlights twice. The Zodiac slows, then, bow forward, comes into the shallows. Richard Sanchez drops into waist-high water, as The Squirrel swings the Zodiac into the open sea again. Richard Sanchez is a machinegun specialist and a trained mechanic in Jet Drive engines. His codename is The Ants.

The Ants comes out of the water and walks towards the pickup. Fleary asks him to join the men in the tray. The Pest drives about two hundred yards up a track running parallel to the shoreline and parks at the secluded campsite, under a large almond tree. Fleary holds a briefing then places the two prisoners under the guns of The Ants, The Iguana and The Thinker. The others pull dry coconut branches under the almond tree, creating a bed. Fleary tells The Thinker to wake him at 0400 hours, and he and the others bed down.

At 0358 hours The Thinker speaks to The Iguana then wakes Fleary, who in turn rouses The Bear. Fleary and The Bear walk to the road where Fleary sits on a fallen coconut stump and lights a cigarette. He offers one to The Bear who declines. They sit there awaiting The Transporter. The mosquitoes are zinging and keep Fleary and The Bear busy.

Fifteen minutes later, they hear a heavy rumbling then see fingers of light penetrating the dark foliage. Suddenly two head-lights burst into full view. The big Transporter pulls up a few feet away. Fleary speaks to The Dove who is driving The Transporter, then walks into the track and signals The Dove. The Transporter makes it way alongside the almond tree. The Dove and others ex-change greetings. All hands are now wide awake.

Quickly they set up camp, tying the tarpaulin from the sides of the truck and staking the other end to the ground creating a lean-to shed. They pull large camouflage nets over the structure. Soon dawn chases the darkness over the sloping eastern hills of Galfa Point.

Fleary and The Pest rustle up a camper's breakfast and signal the Zodiac. The Zodiac comes to shore. The Squirrel disembarks then takes breakfast to the two men onboard, and the Zodiac is taken back to anchorage. The Squirrel remains on shore. The men sit around the fire, chatting and eating then the three ECU men who came on The Transporter with The Dove take over the guard-ing of the prisoners. The Thinker, Iguana and Ants have breakfast. The men then take the sleeping bags out of The Transporter and spread them in the camp. Fleary holds a briefing, then all hands, except Fleary and the three guards, crawl into bed. Fleary walks to the beach, takes the notebook and pen out of his pocket, sticks the pen behind his right ear and sits on a large boulder near the water's edge. It's time to choose the assault team.

He sits deep in thought, like a football coach trying to select his best players to confront the opposition. On missions like this, The Pest is team leader. But there is the emotional aspect. No commander would send The Pest on this raid, but Fleary knows him. He had worked alongside The Pest on many a mission and knew that once he swung into action he was disciplined and emotion-free, a seasoned professional. Fleary would break with conventionalism here: The Pest would go along as the boat handler. He was the best damn small boat operator in the ECU and he knew the Macareo River. The Thinker would be team leader on this one. Fleary writes:

Assault Team: The Thinker: room-clearer and team leader; The Hawk: room-clearer; The Dove: room-clearer and medic; The Bear: room-clearer; The Iguana: sniper and intelligence officer; The Squirrel: spotter and additional sniper; The Ants: machine gunner and mechanic; The Pest: boat handler and navigation officer.

With the team chosen, Fleary heads back to camp and recovers his sketch from the pickup. In The Transporter there is a map of the Macareo. He calls for Pompey. Fleary sits on a large, dried coconut. Pompey sits on the ground in a lotus position opposite Fleary, his hands still handcuffed behind his back; the guard is off to the side. Fleary grills him for over an hour, recording the vitals. The facts are consistent with Pompey's earlier information. The morning sunlight casts its rays upon Pompey's face; he blinks. Fleary observes him: the creases on his face betray worry. Fleary places a cigarette between Pompey's lips (he grunts in gratitude) and allows him to smoke. Fleary signals to the guard: take him away. Armed with the map and sketch, Fleary takes his selected eight on the beach for a stroll, leaving the others behind to prepare lunch and guard the prisoners.

'Gentlemen, we are about to embark on a very sensitive mission that could have implications. We are taking a long shot and going into Venezuela to rescue The Pest's daughter. I have chosen eight of you but if anyone wishes exemption raise your hand.' Fleary waits. All hands are down. He nods in appreciation. He scans the surroundings: the anchored Zodiac bobs off the coast; along the stretch of shore, in either direction, pelicans stand drying their wings.

Fleary picks up a twig and snaps the end. The receding tide has left the perfect grainy blackboard. Fleary has two men hold the map as he squats and draws in the sand. He puts in the south coast, sticks in Galfa Point then traces the Venezuelan coastline, the Macareo river; up river he indicates Wapowa, the Indian Village; up Ghost River there is the bend, then on the left bank the hideout with the two buildings, the walkway and the jetty.

Fleary steps back, looks at his handiwork and smiles. With inputs from the men, he recaps minute details of the impending raid until everyone is clear about *their* function on the mission. He erases the drawing with his boot and they head back to camp.

Back at camp lunch is ready. They eat, signal the Zodiac and beach the vessel. The sailors from the Zodiac have lunch, while the others offload The Transporter and tote the equipment down to the beach. Under Fleary's scrutinising gaze, they prepare the Zodiac for battle. The Ants guides the team in mounting the general purpose machinegun at the stern. All arms, ammunitions and equipment are stored in quick-to-grab areas. Each man has a space for his personal gear.

'That medical kit,' Fleary asks, 'is it properly stocked?'

'Yes, sir,' The Dove says. 'I checked it up at the Transporter.'

'Double check that it has IV.'

The Dove skips to the bow and opens the kit. 'Yes, sir.'

'Very good, carry on.'

The team launches the Zodiac and The Pest takes her out for a trial run. A few adjustments and she is properly trimmed. Back onshore, they refuel the Zodiac. After eating, the two sailors return the Zodiac to anchorage, with instructions to return to shore at 2200 hours. The men have a swim in the sea. At 1600 hours, Fleary tells the team to get some shuteye.

At 1800 hours, Fleary calls ECU Headquarters requesting the chopper, the ECU doctor and two additional ECU men. At 1900 hours the chopper lands where the grass ends and the shore begins, and remains standby. At 2000 hours the men have dinner and Fleary holds his final briefing, painstakingly going over the details of the raid. At 2200 hours the Zodiac comes ashore and the assault team takes over from the ECU sailors onboard. The Pest throttles her slowly into deeper water, then up to full speed. Stand-

ing onshore, Fleary sees the shimmering white serpent in the Zodiac's wake as she screams away into the dark night. He whispers a
prayer.

The sea is calm, and The Pest has The Zodiac running at breakneck
speed. Quickly, they are into Venezuelan territorial waters. The
men are on full alert. The Thinker and The Hawk are on the bow,
their guns ready. The Ants mans the machinegun at the stern, praying for the non presence of a Guardia vessel. They are nearing the
mainland. The quarter moon is floating high over the silhouetted
wall of mangrove, like a silver banana in the sky, as they enter the
big mouth of the Macareo.

The Pest steers the Zodiac to the left bank to avoid the
small fishing settlement on the other side. Pompey had told them
of the occasional presence of the National Guard on the settlement, therefore The Pest, taking no chances, keeps her close to the
left bank. They are into the river now and The Pest has her at full
stretch. The river looks like a huge sheet of darkly-tinted glass, with
the moon's silver streak in the middle. The Pest sticks to the left, as
the map had shown sandbanks on the right when going up river.

Into the night they speed. The Pest weaves between canoes
filled with indigenous Indians doing night fishing. The Ants, man-
ning the gun at the stern, observes the backwash and pities the Wa-
rahoons. Onward they go, silent men, alert going-to-war men, warriors perhaps with hidden thoughts of loved ones left behind, fami-
lies to get back to, men traversing the night at a desperate speed.
The Pest sees lights off his starboard bow. They are approaching
Wapowa, the tiny Indian village. Still at top speed, he inches closer
to the left bank and after they pass the village, he switches sides,
slows and they begin looking for Ghost River.

In Ghost River, The Pest slows to idle speed. The Zodiac is
almost silent. A few hundred feet off the bend The Thinker raises
his hand. The Pest cuts the engine, everyone dons Night Vision
Goggles, switches on their headphones and they begin to paddle.
Stealthily, they head for the right bank where The Iguana and The
Squirrel jump out with their equipment. These two would work

their way along the bank until opposite the hideout and set up their observation nest. Their job is to ascertain which building the girl is in.

The Zodiac is paddled to the left bank and camouflaged. The four room clearers collect their equipment and work their way towards the back of the hideout, while The Pest and Ants hide in the Zodiac.

Already The Iguana and Squirrel are clawing their way trying to get opposite the hideout, but the going is sticky in the dark. They move from mangrove root to mangrove root with their heavy equipment. Mosquitoes are swarming all around, but they press on stubbornly. Already, they could see lights in the hideout. They creep on. They hear voices, and obliquely opposite the hideout they encounter a clump of bush. *Here* they set up a sniper's nest. The surveillance begins.

Meanwhile, the room-clearers are inching their way around the bend on the other side of the river. They head inland then double back until fifty feet behind the hideout.

The Thinker whispers into his headphone: 'Come in, Iguana.'

'Iguana here.'

'Update.'

'Already in position. Two guards out front on the walkway adjoining the two buildings. Nothing on the girl as yet.'

'Does everything out front look like what we have on the sketch?'

'Yes, the jetty is about forty five feet. From our position the boat is moored on the right side of the jetty.'

'Okay, Iguana, standby.' The Thinker asks, 'Pest, did you copy?'

'Yes, skipper.' The Pest is standing by with The Ants in the Zodiac.

Sixty-five minutes has passed since The Iguana and The Squirrel began their surveillance. They are still in their nest opposite the hideout. No sign of the girl but they are patient. They know of the five men in the larger building, the two guards on the walkway. They have heard low voices in the smaller building but nothing else. The Squirrel brushes mosquitoes off his Night Vision Goggles. A man exits the larger building and thumps along the walkway. He passes the guards and playfully taps one on the head. He opens the door of the smaller building and enters. The door remains open. The Squirrel elbows The Iguana. Both look intently through their scopes.

A girl screams and runs through the door of the smaller building and onto the walkway. Her hands are tied behind her back. The man rushes out and grabs her, pulling her into the room. He shoves her to the floor in the right corner. Someone confronts the assailant. They gesture as if cursing each other in Spanish. The door is still open. The Iguana sees the girl. She is still on the floor as the men jostle closer to the door. The first man exits, slams the door and mopes back to the larger building.

'Come in, Thinker,' says The Iguana.

'Thinker here.'

'There's a girl in the smaller building. Looks like the subject, but can't be sure. From where we are she is in the right side of the building.'

'Good, that means she's away from the door. How many enemy personnel have you observed so far?'

'There are at least five in the larger building and two guards out front. We can confirm one man in the smaller building with the girl, but we've picked up low whispers inside, so there's sure to be more.'

'Are you copying this transmission, Pest?' asks The Thinker.

'Yes, skipper.'

'Okay, men, we are moving towards the back door for breaching. Iguana, as soon as I give the word, the two guards belong to you and The Squirrel. Pest, the larger building is yours and The Ants. Do you all copy?'

'Copy,' says The Iguana.

'Copy, skipper.' The Pest and The Ants remove the camouflage from the Zodiac.

The room-clearers creep into position at the back door. The Thinker whispers into the headphones:

'Ready, snipers?'

'Ready.'

'Are you there, Pest?' asks The Thinker.

'Ready, skipper.'

'Okay, Pest, the first shot gets you into position.'

'Copy.'

On the walkway, two guards amble down the jetty. One removes a pack of cigarettes out of his pocket. He taps out two and passes one to his partner who sticks it between his lips. The first guard dips into his pocket again and comes up with a cigarette lighter. He presses the flint and the flame emerges. He cups the flame with both hands against the wind and carries it towards his partner's cigarette.

The Thinker commands: 'Snipers, take them out.'

The Iguana and The Squirrel exhale; their Parker Hale sniper rifles shatter the night – the cigarette lighter leaps into the air and hisses as it falls into the water. The guards fall against each other, embrace and crumble on the jetty; the assault team is already breaching the back door of the smaller building. The Pest launches the Zodiac at full throttle; she swoops down on the hideout. Expertly, The Pest swings her around, bearing the Zodiac's stern on the larger building. The Ants strafes the bigger building with his machinegun. Screams of agony pierce the night, as The Ants hammers away, dealing death across the border. Splinters fly everywhere. A man dives through a window, but The Ants catches him in midair; chunks of flesh cascade into the murky water.

With the backdoor breached, The Thinker, Hawk, Bear and Dove swing into action in the smaller building. A stun grenade is thrown inside, a flash, a bang. A man rises from a hammock. The Thinker's UZI is on semiautomatic; he presses the trigger ever so lightly, and the man slumps back into the hammock.

The Bear's head and gun swing from left to right. 'I see the girl,' he yells.

'Secure her!' roars The Thinker. To his right a head sticks out from a double-decker bunk. The Thinker switches to automatic and sweeps the bunk with an acrid volley.

The Bear reaches the girl. A quick glance confirms *it is* Ayana. He yanks her down and covers her with his body. A hostile figure is coming through the breached door, but The Dove takes him out with a single shot. Someone is high up in a hammock close to the roof. He's reaching for something on a shelf against the wall; The Hawk sees him and takes him out in a flash. The room is clear. Outside, The Ants is still hammering the second building.

The Thinker is on the headphone. 'We got the girl. Is the front clear? Do you read, Pest? Do you read, snipers?'

'Standby, skipper!' The Pest warns. 'We're working on the larger building!'

The Ants changes the machinegun barrel, loads another magazine and sweeps the building with repeated volleys; wooden splinters fly everywhere. The Pest scans the area: no sign of life.

'All clear on my side, Iguana, how about you?' asks The Pest. The Iguana and Squirrel take one last careful scan. They are covering the angles with their rifles and they give the all clear. 'You can come out now,' said The Iguana.

'Okay, we're on our way,' says The Thinker.

The Pest throttles the Zodiac and brings it alongside the jetty. The Thinker exits first, his UZI ready. The Bear appears, clutching the girl like a baby. The Hawk and The Dove cover them. The Thinker skips over the two dead bodies, as The Bear, shielding the girl's face, moves around them. The Hawk and The Dove are right on their heels. The Thinker jumps into the Zodiac. The Bear passes the girl to him and gets in. The Hawk and The Dove follow. They are all in.

The Pest spins the Zodiac in a vicious arc. The Hawk pulls a grenade and hurls it into the boat on the other side of the jetty as they dart to the opposite bank to retrieve the snipers. There is an explosion and flames engulf the boat. The Zodiac closes in on The Iguana and Squirrel, already out of their nest and running towards the bank. They still wear their Night Vision Goggles. Suddenly,

The Iguana catches the glint of a rifle's barrel on a tree at the back of the hideout. He stops in his tracks, sees the owner of the rifle, takes aim and fires; simultaneously, the gun in the tree barks. Bullets cross each other's path, both on destructive courses. The Hawk, on the port bow of the Zodiac, lurches forward and stumbles. The Bear grabs him and lays him flat in the boat. The Iguana, seeing his target tumble from the tree, turns towards the Zodiac. The Squirrel is in front. The Zodiac is against the bank. Both men dive in and The Pest has her off and running. He takes the bend and straightens. At top speed, the Zodiac skims Ghost River towards the Macareo.

The Thinker passes the girl to The Squirrel who keeps her down in the middle of the boat. Already The Dove has cut away the garment from The Hawk's wound. He is conscious but bleeding heavily. The Bear holds his flashlight on the wound while The Dove works feverishly to stem the flow of blood. Out into the open Macareo, they swing, leaving Ghost River behind. The Pest takes her close to the right bank to avoid Wapowa Village. The Pest sees a light directly ahead. He veers to the left and speeds past a vessel. A man curses in Spanish. The Dove hooks up an IV bag to The Hawk. The Bear, holding up the IV with his left hand, follows The Dove's every move with his torchlight.

The Pest glances at his Ayana. He longs to hold her, talk to her, reassure her, but not now. His job is to get them out and at the speed they are travelling, with the many turns and twists of the river, a personal distraction could mean disaster. The Ants is at the stern's machinegun, eyeing the wake for threats. The Thinker and Iguana are at the bow, scanning the river, their weapons ready. Down the river they go at nerve-wracking speed. The river mouth widens. The Pest navigates close to the right bank to avoid a settlement.

The Zodiac jumps as they enter the open sea. The Dove steadies The Hawk. The Pest, thinking of The Hawk, maintains a course where the waves least impact the Zodiac. The Thinker looks at his watch: in ten minutes they would be back in Trinidad waters. Fleary had cautioned him about cross border calls. He would wait.

Fleary and his crew would have enough time to consolidate and ready the chopper. The Pest maintains a blistering pace; time is everything. The Thinker scans his watch: nine minutes since they entered the sea. He secures his weapon and radios:

'Galfa Base, Galfa Base, come in to the Zodiac.'

Fleary is waiting. 'Galfa Base receiving, come in Zodiac.'

'Galfa Base, mission accomplished. We have the girl. The Hawk is injured. Have the chopper ready to fly.'

Fleary frowns. 'Is The Hawk critical?'

'No, The Dove thinks it's just a flesh wound. Clean entry and exit, lost some blood though.'

'ETA?'

'Ten minutes,' replies The Thinker.

'Okay, standing by for your arrival, over and out.'

Fleary goes to the chopper pilot. 'They are coming in with a wounded man aboard, ETA ten minutes, better crank it up. Where's doc?'

'He is with the guys on the beach,' says the pilot.

Fleary takes an infrared signalling torch to the beach where the doctor is with other ECU men, smoking.

'They're coming in less than ten minutes,' says Fleary. 'They got the girl but The Hawk is injured. Doc, you got the blood specs for The Hawk?'

'Yeah.'

'Then make advanced preparations.'

'On it.' The doctor hurries to the camp.

Fleary accepts a lighted cigarette from one of his men. Behind him, the helicopter warms up. Fleary walks to the water, feeling concern tinged with relief. With the torch, he gives three quick blinks. He hears the distant drone of the Zodiac's engines. Three more blinks. The drone intensifies until he sees the Zodiac's spray. Three more blinks and she appears.

Men scamper in the water as the Zodiac throttles into shallow ground. The Pest cuts the engines. The Ants and Thinker jump out. The Zodiac is pulled ashore. The Pest pulls off his ski mask and gingerly takes his daughter from The Squirrel.

The Thinker and The Bear get The Hawk into the helicopter. The Pest, Ayana, the doctor, The Dove and Fleary climb aboard.

'Thinker,' Fleary shouts, above the noise of the rotor, 'you and your men will stay behind and demobilize.'

Keeping low, The Thinker shouts back, 'What about the prisoners?'

'Drop Manny off before Bonasse Village.'

'And Pompey?'

'Leave him in Galfa Point,' Fleary barks.

The helicopter lifts off, on its way to the ECU hospital. The Pest leans over to Fleary and says: 'Thank you, sir.'

Fleary smiles. 'I know you would have done the same for me.'

'Guess this one will take a lot of explaining.'

Fleary pats The Pest on his shoulder. 'Nothing to worry about, my friend, the hardest part is done. There are ways of handling the rest, as you would know.'

Two days later the daily newspaper carries the caption:

'Abducted girl found wandering lonely south coast beach, unharmed!'

Three days later, in Venezuela, a newspaper in Tucupita, a remote jungle town, carries a story on its front page; translated into English it reads:

'Nine bodies found in and around a hideout of noted gang leader, Antonio Vargas, alias El Cuchillo. Detectives believe it was gang-related with factions warring for control of turf in the Orinoco Delta Region. El Cuchillo was not among the dead.'

Let the baby come

McDougal, my father, was a Scotsman, who in his youth ran away from Scotland and became a wandering sailor. In his late twenties, he sailed into Trinidad on a ship called The Mid Atlantic. He jumped ship in Port of Spain and signed on as an able-bodied seaman on The Misfit, a cargo ship that was sailing for the Demerara River in British Guyana. The name was quite a testimony to the ship, and the crew too, and a few hours after leaving Port of Spain, about two o'clock in the morning, she ran aground on the reef off Point Rouge. The Misfit began to break up against the reef, and the captain, who was drunk at the time, grabbed up the loud hailer and shouted:

'Every man to himself and the devil take the hindmost.'

The Misfit's crew got the one lifeboat into the water and promptly began fighting over the right to be in it. McDougal, who wasn't as drunk as the captain, decided to take his chances elsewhere; there was an old wooden pallet on the deck. He threw this into the water, dropped his bag on it, jumped into the sea and clung to the pallet as it drifted off the wreckage.

Daylight revealed to McDougal that he was just about two hundred yards off a coastal village. Still on the pallet and lying on his stomach, he paddled with his hands until he got into shallow waters, then he took off his bag, abandoned the pallet and waded to shore. He made land right next to the old jetty in the village of

Bonasse and apparently the remainder of the crew miraculously made it safely to shore near the village of Granville. I understand that the same morning of his arrival in Bonasse, McDougal lay eyes on my mother, and decided he wasn't going back to sea again.

White people was scarce in Bonasse in those days – as far as I hear, you could of count the amount of them living there without disturbing your index finger and thumb. So when my mother, a tall East Indian girl with a straight nose, high cheekbones and long flowing hair, married my father, I hear she started putting on "airs" and began distancing herself from the other villagers just because she married a white man. But it didn't take long for the villagers to have a good laugh at her, because everyone soon found out that McDougal, with his flaming red beard and pirate looks, was just a lazy fellow with a tenderness in his heart for the village rumshops. Really, he was no different to the other men in the village except for his outward appearance and the fact that he smoked pipe while they smoked cigarettes.

I came along about one year after the wedding and another two years later on, as far as I hear, along came another boy, but he died at childbirth, and like he foul up the machinery, because after that my mother didn't make any more children. I grew up very sheltered, because my earliest memories were of me standing by the front gate every morning, watching the children going to school and wishing that I could join them so I could play with them. At the age of five I got my chance, and before I left the house with my father I can still remember my mother saying to me:

'Stokely, I don't want you mixing with them black children. You hear?'

My father, who was smoking his pipe, blew out a puff of smoke and turned to her. 'Now that's silly. Were we not all created by the same God?' My mother's upper lip stiffened and she walked back inside.

Well boy, I didn't take her on at all. After five years of solitary confinement, I couldn't wait. As soon as I walk through the school gate I start to make friends right away. My classmates taught me how to pitch marbles, play hoop, police and thief, and a series of other games. I became one of them and was as happy as can be. We shared everything that we ate: touloum, tamarind ball, green mangoes with pepper and salt, and Jem – a spongy, deliciously sweet, white ball that formed on the inside of a young, growing coconut. I loved my classmates as if they were my own brothers and sisters, and I was sure that they felt the same way about me. One day (I was about eleven years old) my mother and I were outside tending to some plants, when Ivy, an old lady who lived across the road from us, came up to our front gate and said to my mother:

'Primatee, the other day I pass by the school and I see that little half becken-egg boy of yours running and misbehaving just like the little black children.'

My mother turned to me. 'Is so?'

'Yes, is so,' Ivy said, 'he even behaving worst than them.'

My mother turned to my father who was sitting in the gallery reading an old newspaper and smoking his pipe. 'McDougal, you hear what Miss Ivy say? I always tell you we shouldn't let the boy mix with the black children.' My father got up and came towards us. I thought he was going to spank me but he turned to my mother instead. 'So what? Are they not wee ones just like him? If I were to think like you, then we ourselves would have never gotten married.' My mother seemed to recoil at his words. She walked away silently and went into the house. From that day on I start to call him The General.

When I was thirteen I began noticing things that had slipped by unnoticed. My mother did all the work while The General just sat around or drank at the village rumshops. She had a few acres of land that her father had left her and she worked her fingers to the bone, planting crops that she sold to a wholesaler who came by every two weeks with an old Bedford truck. She was the bread winner of the house. Every cent that she made was spent on The General and me. She never complained, and when The General came home drunk and sang to us his native songs of Scotland, her features would light up as she listened to her man, her White Man, her trophy that she had won fair and square, who had given her a son almost his colour. I could almost see in her eyes what she was thinking: if only her parents were still alive to see. And what could I say about The General? Aside from the alcohol, which over the years seemed to have evaporated any ambition he might have had as a young man, The General had his good points too: he genuinely liked people and he didn't have a racial bone in his body.

By the time I was eighteen, I get tall and straight like an arrow. That same year I start to kick ball for a Bonasse football team called Black Hands. My mother didn't like the team; she said the name didn't sound nice. But when I stride out on the Cedros Recreation ground to play for my team, all them black girls whistling me from the crowd and if I tell you what, I had a genuine respect and admiration for all of them. It didn't take long for me to start to fraternise with them and when my mother get *the s* (story) she nearly hit the roof. One night I come in late and I stand right behind the door and I hear her telling The General:

'McDougal, you better start to help me in the garden for we to make some fast money. Let we make haste and send the boy overseas before he bring home a *Capar* daughter-in-law for we.'

Boy, I couldn't believe my ears, I couldn't believe my mother would a use a word like that: you know what is a Capar? A Capar is a derogatory word for a black person, and most of my friends were Creoles. Boy I want to go in there and mash up the place, but something that I read in the past stop me: 'Honour thy mother and father even in times when they don't appear too honorable.'

The General coughed. 'I have no problem if my lad chooses a black daughter-in-law for me.'

But, believe it or not, about one week later, The General started to toil along with Primatee in the garden. I was relieved that night to hear him say to my mother, 'I am helping you because I think it's a good idea for the lad to go away and get an education, nothing else.' Primatee didn't say a word. It was strange to see The General toiling in the hot sun day after day, and I was touched to know that he was doing it for me. He ceased going to the rumshops during the week and the men he used to hang out with made it their duty to pass by and voice their opinion on a daily basis:

'McDougal, you letting that coolie woman domesticate you. Leave she let she work the land and let we go down by Poon Wai and beat some liquor!'

He'd dismiss them with a friendly wave, but Primatee would always respond loud enough for only McDougal to hear: 'Is why I don't like black people. Don't want to do nothing good for they own children. But if they see somebody trying to do for theirs they try to discourage them!'

After a year of great sacrifice my parents sent me overseas, The General because he wanted me to get a better education, Primatee because I suspected she wanted a white daughter-in-law, and she thought that the chances were much better out there. When I get to New York I marvel because it have all the peoples of all the countries of the world: Indians, Chinese, Africans, Europeans, Bajan, South Americans; you name it they have it. And talk about girls! In no time at all I start getting my fair share of the action. I going to school in the day, holding down a lil waiter job in the evening and in the night I between the blanket and the sheet with nice girls from all corners of the globe.

I have to tell you though it is still the black girls that have me mesmerised. They more loving and caring. One day I skip a class and was hurrying over to the bank to cash a cheque that my parents had sent when I see this darkie coming towards me. She was tall and femininely designed and she walked with the type of rhythm that shouted Caribbean product. I watched her coming, beautiful, with her neat Afro hairstyle, and when we were almost alongside, our eyes met and she smiled, the most sincere smile I'd ever seen – not to mention the lovely white teeth. I stopped in my tracks and watched her go by. She looked back and smiled that mesmerising smile again, and I just stood there spellbound. It took a while for me to gather my thoughts. I turned and raced after her, trying to keep track of that Afro hairstyle in the crowd and rehearsing in my mind what I would say to her. When I caught up, I touched her shoulder and when she looked back, all my rehearsals went to naught for my mouth was dry and words wouldn't come. She smiled encouragingly and my tongue loosened a bit. Rebecca, the darkie, was from Antigua. We exchanged names, addresses and telephone numbers and I rushed off to the bank.

We began calling each other regularly and when we started to date, boy, we was like two lost sheep that had found each other in a foreign pasture. It didn't take long for the both of us to realise that there was no getting over each other so we decided that before we end up committing sin, we should get married. It was a quickly arranged, simple ceremony with a few of Rebecca's friends and family and a few of my friends. Rebecca moved into my little apartment.

After the wedding I wrote home and told them that I had gotten married to a girl named Rebecca – no more details – and we would be coming home in three months time after I completed my schooling. Well, boy, I don't know if the name Rebecca have some sort of Caucasian ring to it, but the letter that come back from Trinidad had a nice fat cheque inside signed by my mother, and in the letter she mentioned that I forget to send a picture, "but from the name alone she could guess that she daughter-in-law was a nice white girl with blue eyes and blonde hair." The enclosed cheque was for we belated honeymoon. Well, boy, I start to laugh, because deep down inside, I feel like I pull a good one on the old lady and I can't wait to reach Trinidad just to see the look on she face when me and she supposedly white daughter-in-law walk off that plane. I laughing so hard that Rebecca left the kitchen, where she was rustling up some dinner, and came to see what was so funny. When she asked, I say to myself, but wait, I can't show my wife this letter, but then I decided to pass it off as a joke:

'Becca, your mother-in-law have a real sense of humour, girl. Watch what she write here in this letter.'

After Rebecca read the letter she said, sarcastically, 'Yes, boy, my mother-in-law have a real sense of humour.'

A piece of reality hit me immediately: it had a great possibility that the two ladies in my life might not hit it off. Trouble is I love them both. Anyway, I am a young fellow with a lot of faith, so I keeping my fingers crossed.

I banish those dreadful thoughts and Rebecca and me change that cheque and put it to the use that it was sent for, a honeymoon. If you see us on the streets of New York like two parakeets. You know what is a parakeet? It is a little green bird that does move around in pairs, always together in the daylight, smooching, and in the night they does fly into a little hole in a tree trunk. During the night they get so close upon each other that in the morning he gets up wearing her feathers and she gets up wearing his. Well, it didn't have any tree in New York with a hole big enough for us to get into, so we use to crawl into our little apartment and, boy, we use to get so close during the night that when we get up in the morning, my wife use to be creamish-red and I use to be black. I know you think I lie, but is true, my woman and I was having a grand time in New York City.

The three months passed quickly. On the airplane with my wife bound for Trinidad, I was hovering between laughter and concern. I couldn't wait to see the look on my mother's face when she saw me and she black daughter-in-law walk off the plane, but still I was apprehensive about what Rebecca's reactions might be to what I thought would be a testing relationship between the two.

The plane landed at the airport, taxied down the runway and stopped in front the waving gallery. After a while the exit ramp was brought alongside the airplane, the door opened and the passengers began to file out. When Rebecca and I stepped into the sunlight, I stood on the exit ramp, took a deep breath and looked up at the waving gallery. I saw The General and my mother standing in front an excited crowd, all gathered there to welcome home loved ones. I placed my left arm around Rebecca and used the other to give my parents a thumbs up signal. The General smiled, but even at that distance I saw my mother's face drop, as she held on to The General's shirtsleeve.

When Rebecca and I cleared customs and met up with my parents, The General greeted his daughter-in-law warmly, but my mother sulked off to the side and refused to acknowledge my wife. That night, at home in Bonasse, I struggled to explain old customs and taboos of the different races in Trinidad to my wife. I assured her that things would only get better between the two of them. But later that night, on my way to the kitchen to get a glass of water, I wasn't so sure when I heard my mother inside her room fretting to The General:

'Imagine we send that bitch half way round the world to get him away from them Capar, and look what he bring back! If I did only know it have Capar up there, I would have send him somewhere else.'

The General said, 'Oh stop making yourself a nuisance. You're becoming an embarrassment.'

I watched my wife trying her utmost to befriend her mother-in-law but my mother ignored her. One month after we arrived home Rebecca came back from a visit to the doctor with good news: she was two months pregnant. That afternoon when my father and I were alone in the gallery I said:

'General, I have good news and bad news.'

'Give me the good one first, laddie.'

'She pregnant,' I said.

The General sucked on his pipe and exhaled sharply, smoke filtering through his now red and grey beard. Then he smiled that contagious smile of his. 'Why that's wonderful, lad.' We sat there for awhile, The General in quiet contemplation. 'And the bad news?'

'Rebecca and me moving out,' I said. 'We don't want the child to born in this racial environment that mammy creating.'

The General was quiet for a long time. 'That would kill your mother, laddie. I suppose I should have raised this topic with you and Rebecca a while ago but I was hoping that things would of sorted themselves out. You see, son, it seems to me that certain people messed up these two races a long time ago, because it was beneficial for them to always have one at the other's throat. Racism is a disease created by misinformation, ignorance and false pride. But it can be cured by us living amongst each other and learning the truth, which is, we are no different from each other. The both of you leaving now will do no good for any of us. Just let the baby come and I guarantee that you will see a complete turnaround in your mother's attitude towards your wife.'

'But General—'

'Hold on a minute and hear me out, lad. Speak to Rebecca and tell her the exact words that I have told you, and I too will continue to press against your mother's conscience. I guarantee you that as soon as Rebecca's belly starts to raise your mother's attitude towards her will change.'

When The General finish, he have my head in a spin but I willing to give it a try. That night I spoke to Rebecca, handing it out to her just as The General laid it out to me, and guess what? She decided to give it a try. You see why I love my wife?

Boy, as Rebecca belly start to rise, I notice that my mother's attitude towards her began to soften. By the time the child born it was a complete turnaround: my mother claiming the child like if she make it — you'd of never guessed that it was my "Capar" woman that give birth to it. I can't even get to hold my own daughter without my mother fussing:

'Doh hold the chile so, you go give it *hassulie*... place you hand under the back and cradle it properly.'

And, boy, she start to treat Rebecca like a spoiled daughter: breakfast in bed and she don't even want her to lift a matchstick. Rebecca was so happy that she gave the child an Indian name; we call her Vashti. I say to myself, boy, The General is a boss, he did really know what he saying.

As time go by the three ladies in my life form a bond that have me blushing with gratitude. As Vashti grew so did her beautiful hair, and The General and my mother just couldn't seem to keep their hands away from those curls. One day I came home from work and standing, opening the front gate, I looked towards the house where I saw the most beautiful picture I have ever seen: on the front step sat my Indian mother, holding an Afro comb, combing the hair of my African wife; on the lower step sat my white father running his hands through the curls of my *dougla* daughter. I say to myself, wait, I belong to a rainbow family and I was glad as hell to be part of it too. Boy, I happy that I did take

The General advice and stick it out, because, I too found out that we are all one people, created by the same Creator, and he does only create first class. All of we first class. So if it have any of you out there, boy or girl, married into a different race and your "in-laws" giving you the same problems that my Rebecca get in the beginning, don't worry, time will heal their prejudice. But if you want to hasten the process, shake the bed and let the baby come.